Ian took the liberty of watching Esther.

Though quiet, she leaned back with her face turned toward the sun. A gentle breeze ruffled her hair, and as she did so often, she reached up and tucked a few loose strands behind her ear.

He watched her pull suntan lotion from her shoulder bag and rub it along her neck and arms to protect her fair skin.

"Would you like some?" she asked, extending the plastic bottle. "I'll put it on for you. Your neck is the most likely to burn, I think."

Ian held his breath, waiting in expectation until her cool hands rested on his skin, glided along his hairline then down his neck. When she was finished, she gave him a playful squeeze.

He loved the feel of her gentle touch on his skin. The intimacy. Most of all, he loved having Esther at his side, bantering like a real friend.

Books by Gail Gaymer Martin

Love Inspired

Upon a Midnight Clear #117
Secrets of the Heart #147
A Love for Safekeeping #161
Loving Treasures #177
Loving Hearts #199

Silhouette Romance

Her Secret Longing #1545
Let's Pretend... #1604

GAIL GAYMER MARTIN

loves so many things—her husband, family, writing, singing and her Lord. She grew up in nearby Madison Heights, Michigan, and now lives with her real-life hero, Bob, in Lathrup Village. Though she'd written all her life—stories, articles for professional journals, skits and poems for fellow teachers and programs for her church—she finally captured her dream of writing professionally after she retired.

Gail is an award-winning, multipublished author in nonfiction and fiction with fourteen novels, five novellas and many more to come. Her Steeple Hill Love Inspired romance, *Upon a Midnight Clear,* won a Holt Medallion in 2001. Besides writing, Gail enjoys singing, public speaking and presenting writers' workshops. She believes that God's gift of humor gets her through even the darkest moment.

She loves to hear from her readers. Write to her at gail@gailmartin.com or at P.O. Box 760063, Lathrup Village, MI 48076.

LOVING
HEARTS

GAIL GAYMER MARTIN

Love Inspired.

Published by Steeple Hill Books™

STEEPLE HILL BOOKS

Steeple Hill™

ISBN 0-373-87206-2

LOVING HEARTS

Copyright © 2003 by Gail Gaymer Martin

Visit us at www.steeplehill.com

Printed in U.S.A.

My purpose is that they may be
encouraged in heart and united in love.
—*Colossians* 2:2

Laban replied: "It is not our custom here to give the younger daughter in marriage before the older one."
—*Genesis* 29:26

To my nieces, Jodi and Andrea,
both with loving husbands,
loving families and loving hearts.

Chapter One

"**Y**ou've cut your hair."

Startled, Esther Downing raised her attention from the pile of books and gaped at Ian Barry's deep blue eyes smiling at her through dark-framed spectacles. "Yes, I had it cut." She'd read his name many times on his library card, but he'd never spoken to her beyond general comments.

"I like it," he said, still focusing on her new style.

"Thanks." Guided by a natural reflex, she brushed her hand down her shorter cut. Pushing her discomfort aside, Esther regained composure. She forced a casual smile. "Can I help you?"

"Sure thing," he said, then hesitated. "You always wore it back in...some kind of a twist."

"Excuse me?"

"Your hair. I like it down and soft around your face. You look..." He smiled. "Nice."

"That's kind," Esther said, addled by his compliment. "Now—" she drew in a calming breath "—what can I do for you?"

A shy grin tugged at his mouth. "I'm looking for a book." His lips parted to a full smile. "I suppose a library is a good place to find one."

She only nodded, totally confused by the chatty dialogue.

"Here," he said, dipping his hand beneath his spring jacket and pulling a folded paper from his shirt pocket. He laid the note on the counter and pointed. "This is what I need."

Esther eyed the list. "*Hull Parameters and Performance?* I'm not sure—"

"For a sailboat," he said. "I'm planning to refurbish an old cutter I bought."

His words sent her on a wave of nostalgia. "I loved to sail…once." Her voice faded with her admission.

"Once?" His eyebrows rose. "I thought sailing was like the circus. It gets in your blood." He rested his arm on the counter.

"Not mine. I had an unc—" Amazed that she had almost burdened a stranger with her past, she stifled her thought.

A faint frown pulled at his features. "Something happened?"

"It's not important. Let me see what—"

"Yes, it is." He gave her forearm a gentle touch.

Esther wavered at the warmth that fired along her skin.

"A boating accident?" he asked, genuine interest reflected in his eyes.

She wished she were able to retract her earlier disclosure. She nodded, feeling the tug of unpleasant memories. "An uncle. My father's brother drowned in a storm on Lake Michigan."

"I'm sorry, Esther."

Esther. His voice sounded gentle and sincere. He'd obviously read her name on the desk nameplate, but he'd never said it before. Today his tender reference caught her by surprise.

"Thanks. It was long ago right here in Loving. We were just kids, but we loved sailing with him. Our whole family."

"You don't sail anymore?" he asked.

She shook her head, feeling a prickle of sadness.

"You should. Remember the old adage. If you fall off a horse, get back on and ride."

She couldn't help but smile. "I don't think I've heard that particular adage."

Ian grinned back. "Someone said something like that. You get the point." He pushed his glasses higher on his nose. "Accidents happen every day. Cars, planes, trains…and boats. We never know when it's our time to go. You can't let someone else's time for heaven stop you from enjoying life."

She shrugged, amazed at the compassion etching his face. And he was right. Her uncle was certainly in heaven. "Let me look up that book for you," she said, needing to get her rattled thoughts in check.

"I'm not sure you'll find a book by that name," he said. "It's more like a topic."

Esther entered the subject into the computer and

ran a search. Nothing. She pinched the bridge of her nose and thought.

"If you can't find that, try hull design or sailboat design," he said, watching the screen.

When she typed in the new subject, a list of books appeared. She grabbed a pen and jotted down the Dewey decimal numbers. "Let me show you where these are located."

When she came from behind the counter and stepped beside him, a faint aroma of tangy citrus enveloped her. She liked the fresh, natural fragrance, which seemed to fit this gentle man.

Short of help in the small library, she often stayed behind the checkout counter and guided the patrons with verbal directions. Today she'd been motivated to lead the way. As they walked side by side, Ian's arm brushed her shoulder. She calculated his size— about four inches taller than her five foot seven. A good-looking man, though his features seemed overpowered by his dark-rimmed glasses.

Drawing her attention from Ian, she checked the cataloging numbers and found the aisle. Moving between the shelves, she located books on sailing. "Here they are." She indicated various volumes that had appeared on her computer screen.

"Thanks," he said, sending her a pleasant smile, "I'll take a look."

She watched him thumb through an index, then select another book before she retreated to her desk, her curiosity aroused. What had caused this sudden burst of friendship? Though Esther knew he was an avid reader and frequented the library often, Ian had always seemed quiet and restrained. Why now did she notice such a change?

Her hand instinctively rose to her hair, and she fondled the blunt ends. Before the cut, she'd worn it in a French twist most of the time. Now the new style had given her a fresh image. When she looked in the mirror, Esther saw a younger, friendlier face. Maybe that's why Ian had behaved differently today.

Esther often—too often, she thought—heard her voice spark with business and sensed an aloofness in her demeanor despite her desire to act otherwise.

She wished she were more like Rachel. Her younger sister found it easy to make friends and talk to strangers. Approachable. That's what Esther longed to be.

From behind the checkout desk she observed Ian carrying a stack of books to a nearby table. From the corner of her eye she watched him slide off his jacket and toss it over the chair back. In contrast to his trim waist, Ian's broad shoulders surprised her. He opened each book and scanned the pages, then put some in one stack and some in another.

Realizing she was ogling, Esther winced while a sinking feeling fluttered through her stomach. Ian smiled her way, and she felt certain he'd caught her staring at him.

Her face burning with mortification, she turned away and busied herself at the computer or checked out books for patrons—anything to avoid looking his way. Usually priding herself on doing her job and keeping herself focused, today she'd never felt so inept.

"I'll take these."

Hearing his voice, Esther jumped, then lassoed her nervous energy and gained control. "Apparently you found something useful," she said, pulling his books forward. "These can be checked out for two months. Two weeks," she corrected.

"Two weeks should do it," he said, resting his hands on the counter edge.

"If you need any more information, we have computers that our visitors can use…to locate books and do their own Internet research. I can show—"

"What I'd really like is to have someone do the work for me," he said.

She studied his face to see if he were serious.

"You don't happen to know anyone who does research, do you?"

Esther's pulse skipped. She wanted to avoid the truth, but she couldn't. "I do. I have my own business."

"Really?" His gaze caught hers.

"Just part-time."

"You're kidding. Here at the library?" he asked.

"No, at home. I have an office there."

"Could I have your business card?"

His question rattled her and a knot worked its way up her back. Befuddled by her reaction, she reached beneath the desk where she kept a few cards and handed him one.

Ian dropped it into his pocket. "Thanks. You might come in handy…I mean, your service."

She nodded while a faint grin settled on her mouth. Pulling her gaze from his, she ran his books through the scanner and placed them in a neat pile. "Here you go."

"Thanks. I wouldn't feel so pressured if I weren't taking vacation time in a couple weeks to get the boat in shape. After the tourist season begins, my job's too hectic." He pulled the books to the edge of the counter and paused.

Realizing he was waiting for her to respond, she asked the question that rose in her mind. "Where do you work?"

"Bay Breeze Resort." His head tilted in the direction of the resort. "On Lake Michigan. I'm the assistant manager under Philip Somerville." Pride registered in his voice.

"Really? My sister's fian...steady works there, too." Fiancé. The word stuck in her throat, reminding her of the eternal problem she had to face.

"Small world. What's his name?"

"Jeff Langley. Do you know him?"

Ian smiled. "Know him? Sure. Jeff's the reception desk manager."

"Maybe you know my sister, then? Rachel Downing. I'm sure he's taken her to some of the staff parties."

"Possibly. I meet so many people." He leaned closer, his tone confidential. "To be honest, I avoid the events when I can."

Surprised, Esther wondered why. Maybe he felt the way she did—not really happy in large crowds. "You'll have to look for Rachel next time."

"I will." He grinned and adjusted his glasses.

"You should come by the resort for dinner some night. Or lunch. You and..."

"Rachel? I might do that." Or did he mean her and a date? His engaging look gave her the jitters. She wished he would be on his way. Though she liked his gentle good nature, his questions and the glint in his eye flustered her.

He gathered the books in his arms and took a step backward. "Thanks for your card. Maybe I'll see you at Bay Breeze sometime."

Maybe not, Esther thought as he walked toward the door. She watched until he vanished, her mind a flutter of confusion. How many men had she helped locate books? For how many customers had she done research? So why had she reacted this way? As the question entered her mind, she'd found the answer. Esther had no interest in befriending a man...especially one compelled to sail.

Despite her feelings, Ian's shy smile swept through her thoughts.

Ian rose from his desk, wadded the wrapper from his sandwich and arched it into the wastebasket. His hunger hadn't subsided, and, remembering Bay Breeze's great desserts, he considered finagling some pie from the restaurant.

The books he'd borrowed from the library the week before lay strewn across his desk, and he gathered them up in a neat pile. He'd found lunch break a convenient time to study the information and jot down some of the details he thought might be useful.

He'd never refurbished a boat before, but the

thought excited him. As a young man he'd sailed with his father and knew the ropes. Yet that didn't mean he could rebuild a cutter. Wishing his father were alive, he imagined how pleasurable it might be to share the experience with him. Another impossible dream.

His vacation would begin in another week, and he prayed he could make the most of his time. He'd rented a slip at the local marina and had the vessel in dry dock. At least he'd made a beginning.

The librarian's image rose in his thoughts. He'd wanted to kick himself when he called her Esther. He'd seen her name on her desk and had secretly let the word roll off his tongue so many times. Esther. The name sounded wholesome and rather old-fashioned. Biblical, he recalled.

Ian had surprised himself last week in the library. Opening his mouth to ask for the books, he'd heard himself talk about her hair…as if he was a stylist. She probably thought he was weird.

Laughing at himself, he drew back his shoulders, deciding he didn't care. He found the woman attractive and, more than that, kind and intelligent. He'd watched her in the library helping children, teenagers and adults. No matter what age or manner, Esther seemed to have the answers they needed. Ian had admired her from afar. But not last week. He'd blatantly fawned over her.

That day, he'd made a mistake. Ian had seen her protective shield rise immediately when he became too familiar. She'd stiffened at his comments instead of enjoying the attention, as he'd hoped she might.

Ian pulled open his desk drawer and eyed Esther's business card. Realizing that he might have use for her services during his month's work on the boat, he pulled out his wallet and slipped the card into one of the credit card slots, then slid the wallet into his back pocket.

Who was he kidding? He had more interest in Esther than in her research. Instead of hiring her, he'd save money by hanging out in the library and doing his own.

For someone thirty-five, he disappointed himself. Why didn't he have the courage to introduce himself, tell Esther he admired her and ask her to dinner? As the question crossed his mind, the answer followed in neon. He'd been brushed off too many times not to be a little punchy about taking the dramatic step forward. Instead, he'd take one small step at a time.

The pie slipped back into his thoughts and Esther's image drifted into a quiet reverie as he started for the dining room. Since tourist season wouldn't begin for another few weeks, the resort restaurant provided a quiet haven for businessmen meeting over lunch and locals celebrating special occasions.

Ian closed his office door, strode through the hotel lobby and into the restaurant. A few diners sat in the hushed room, and he headed for the work station to order his pie. Before he reached his destination, he faltered and peered ahead at the two blond women seated in the middle of the room.

The one facing him looked vaguely familiar. Observing them, Ian saw her animated face blossom into a bright smile. Earlier, her breezy chuckle had caught his attention, but it wasn't her laugh or smile that kept him riveted. The woman facing away had nudged his recollection. Her flaxen-streaked hair had been pushed behind her ear and curved at the nape of her neck. Could it be *her?*

Ian hesitated. Still his curiosity wouldn't subside, and instead of walking directly toward the kitchen, he passed the women, squeezed between two empty tables and gazed out the window before turning to face her. *Esther.* He'd been right.

Capturing his confidence, he approached her. "Hello," he said. "I see you took my advice."

Her eyes darted from his face to the woman across from her before she sent him a faint smile.

"Yes, my sister asked me to lunch," she said. "I didn't think I'd see you on a Saturday."

The comment crushed his confidence like a highway stone smacking his windshield. Had she hoped to avoid seeing him? At least she'd admitted thinking about him. "I work some Saturdays," he said, covering his confusion.

He turned his attention to her tablemate. "You're Rachel, if I remember correctly."

She nodded, her eyes shifting to Esther and back before she extended her hand. "Yes, and you are…?"

He grasped her palm in his. "Ian Barry. I have a library card."

"Congratulations," she said, following this with a girlish giggle.

Great impression, he chided himself. "I mean, that's how I know your sister." He let her hand slip from his. "Esther mentioned you're Jeff Langley's friend?"

She grinned. "Mmm-hmm. He's working today."

"Is this a special occasion?" Ian asked, motioning toward their lunch plates.

Esther shook her head. "No. Nothing like that."

"I see." Her response left him with a go-nowhere feeling. He scuffled for something else to say. "The books have been helpful."

"That's my job," she said.

Though he sensed her dismissal, he didn't move. "I have my cutter dry-docked at the municipal marina."

"Sounds like you're making progress," she said.

"Yes, I am." Words. None came…until he eyed her plate. "How was lunch?" The mundane question fell from his lips.

"Excellent," Rachel said. "I had the salmon."

"It's fresh. Caught right here," he said, gesturing toward the lake. He couldn't believe he was standing there discussing fish with Esther's sister when all he wanted to do was talk with Esther.

Struck by a thought, he flinched at his lack of tact. Maybe he'd interrupted an important, even serious, conversation.

"Is this part of your job…finding out how the clientele enjoys the food?" Esther asked, a faint grin curving her pink lips.

Her smile encouraged him. "That, among other things."

"The room has a nice view," she said, motioning

toward the wall of windows. "I imagine the sunsets are beautiful."

With her chin tilted upward and her gray eyes directed at his, he couldn't recall the sunsets. He only saw her lovely face. "They are," he said finally.

The air filled with awkward silence, so without further delay, Ian said goodbye and backed away, feeling unnaturally inept at conversation. His desire for pie had been dashed.

Esther sat unmoved for a moment, then glanced over her shoulder in time to see Ian pass through the doorway. She wondered why he'd come into the restaurant in the first place.

"Not bad," Rachel said.

Esther swung back toward her sister. "What?"

"He's nice looking...and friendly."

"Yes, he is." Esther steadied herself for what would come next. Their conversation seemed to slip into a pattern each time they were together.

"I don't understand why you're so standoffish with men, Esther. Obviously the man was trying to be friendly, and you acted like he was...a leper." Rachel's face was pinched with irritation.

Esther flinched. "I didn't treat him any such way."

"The poor guy was trying to make conversation. You gave him two-word responses. I don't call that friendly."

"You're different than I am. Just because we're sisters doesn't mean we're clones, Rachel." Watching her sister's hurt expression, Esther wished she could retract her words. "I'm sorry, but there's nothing I can do about my personality."

"Yes, there is, and you know it. I'm tired of keeping my engagement a secret from Dad. Jeff asked me to marry him and bought the ring. I want to wear it. If you don't do something, Esther, you're going to ruin my life."

Chapter Two

Esther gaped at her sister. Rachel's words tore through her. What could she do? Her plans didn't include marriage. And their father...well...he was being unreasonable.

"I'm sorry, Esther," Rachel said, her voice a plaintive whisper. "I didn't mean to attack you. It's Father. He's being—"

"Irrational," Esther finished. "Ridiculous. Old-world. Old Testament. He's making no sense."

"I know...and that's why I'm so frustrated." Rachel brushed tears from her lower lashes. "I've talked to him, and he won't listen." She grasped Esther's hand. "Will you speak with him?"

"About what? He's as determined and stubborn as a trampling herd. There's no stopping him. We've both talked until we're hoarse."

"But it's not fair," Rachel said, her voice trembling with harnessed emotion. "Jeff's been as patient as any man can be. Maybe more so."

Esther crumpled against the chair and knotted the linen napkin on her lap. "Father's not considering my wishes, either. He's attempting to manipulate me through you."

"Why don't you want to get married, Esther? Mom and Dad had a good life. What are you afraid of?"

Esther's gaze shot upward. "I'm not afraid of anything. Good gracious, Rachel. Is fear the only reason not to marry?" Esther's mind tumbled with excuses.

Rachel cleared her throat. "No…I suppose not. Nuns don't marry because of their beliefs, but…"

"I'm not a nun. I'm a single career woman. Why can't Father understand that?" Esther softened her voice, realizing it had reached a few decibels higher than she'd expected. She cringed as heads turned in her direction.

"Has anyone asked you out?" Rachel eyed her a moment before her cheeks turned a pale pink. "I mean…lately."

"What difference does it make if someone has or hasn't?" Esther knew the difference. And no one had…but that was only part of it. She'd rarely been asked on a date in her younger years. Too quiet, she figured. Then after Uncle Jim died in the storm and Esther watched her aunt suffer alone with the kids, she didn't care about marriage.

Perhaps she'd been too impressionable back then, but after her mother died and she witnessed her father's inconsolable grief, her decision had been validated. Loving meant she would risk losing someone…risk being hurt again.

"You mean you wouldn't marry if someone...?" Rachel's voice faltered.

Arching an eyebrow to its limit, Esther glowered at her sister's mottled face. "I realize God instituted marriage. 'Bone of my bones, flesh of my flesh...' But some bones and flesh plan to stay single. Alone. Unattached."

Rachel flinched, and Esther resolved to soften her tone again.

"You're as stubborn as Father," Rachel said. "You won't even give a man a chance."

Agreeing to lunch with Rachel hadn't been Esther's wisest decision. Lately their conversation always turned to her sister's predicament, and that's where Esther preferred it to remain—Rachel's problem, not hers.

Esther drew in a lengthy breath. "I don't understand why you can't marry before I do. That's if I ever do...." Her words faded, and she unclamped her tense jaw. "I'll talk with Dad—again—if it will make you feel better. But it won't do any good."

Despite Esther's final warning, Rachel's face brightened, and she turned her attention to her glass of lemonade.

Esther couldn't concentrate on anything except her quiet misery. She'd spoken to her father many times before about nearly the same subject.

When she and Rachel were younger, he'd insisted that Esther date first. Esther had to do everything before Rachel. She'd spent her life doing things she didn't want so that Rachel could do what she wanted. And each time they tried to reason, Uriah Downing told them the story of Laban in the Old Testament…often with a twist.

No matter how much Rachel explained that the birth of Jesus had given the world the New Testament teachings as well as the Old, her father only pooh-poohed her efforts. Uriah, like a mountain, wouldn't budge.

A mountain? Esther shivered with the thought. The Bible taught that faith could move mountains. Could faith move Uriah Downing? Unless Esther wanted to be responsible for Rachel's spinsterhood, she needed to try a new tactic. And she definitely needed God's help.

Ian stood just inside the library door, speculating what he should do. Besides taking care of his research, he'd come to the library to see Esther, but she was nowhere in sight. He wondered if it might be her day off.

With one final sweep of the room, he retreated outside into the spring sunshine, stirred by disappointment. Bounding down the four slab steps, he pivoted toward the parking lot and found himself face-to-face with Esther. "Es…ther," he said, finding his tongue tangled around her name.

She drew back for a moment until recognition or controlled surprise allowed her to speak. "Ian."

"I thought…" He caught himself. "Where did you come from?"

"The side door," she said. "Were you in the library? I didn't see you."

Ian sensed something was wrong. A dark frown

furrowed her usual smooth forehead and her natural smile seemed strained. "No, I...well..." He struggled with his response. No way could he tell her he'd left the library when he didn't see her there. Instead, a question surged in his thoughts. "You're not through working today?"

"No, it's lunchtime. I needed some air." A sigh rattled from her throat.

"Lunch." Ian grasped the opportunity. "Isn't that a coincidence. I was heading inside when my stomach won out over my research." He tilted back on his heels, pleased that he'd thought so quickly. "Care to join me?"

Esther faltered for a moment, fidgeting with her shoulder-bag strap. "I suppose...yes, I guess not eating alone would be nice for a change."

"I'd enjoy the company," Ian said, the first truth he'd uttered in the past few seconds. "How about the deli on Sixth Street?" He gestured toward the diner.

She agreed and fell into step at his side. After a stretch of uncomfortable silence, Esther lifted her gaze from the sidewalk and looked his way. "You're on vacation?"

"Next week," he said, admiring the way the sunlight played on her hair. "I'm hearing too many ideas on how to refurbish my boat. I decided to read some unbiased viewpoints."

"Objective opinions?" She nodded, a knowing look spreading across her face. "Some people get a conviction stuck in their heads and no matter what you do, you can't budge it."

Ian eyed her, wondering if she were talking about people in general or someone specific. Her tone had been weighted with meaning. Curious as he was, he sensed he'd be wiser not asking. Maybe at lunch she'd tell him what troubled her.

In a few blocks they reached the diner, and once he made his selection, Ian lowered his menu and enjoyed a private moment to admire Esther. Her fair skin appeared translucent in the sunlight filtering through the storefront window. As she scanned the fare, her tinted lips parted. When she lifted her gaze, her gray eyes reflected the soft blue of her simple stonewashed denim dress—like an overcast day that brightens for a moment with a break in the clouds.

"I'm not really hungry," she said, sliding the menu onto the table. "Nothing looks appetizing."

"Chicken noodle soup when you're not feeling well," Ian said, pointing to the feature for the day. "My mom always told me it was good for what ails you."

His comment roused a faint smile on her lips, but he still longed to know what troubled her.

"Sorry, I suppose I'm a bit depressed today," she said. "I've been dealing with a family situa—" She shook her head. "We don't need to get into that."

He eyed the furrow of concern on her face. "Why not? You just mentioned unbiased opinions. Who can give you better counsel than an uninvolved party? Try me."

Her downcast eyes inched upward, and when they settled on his, Ian's pulse tripped. He longed to take her hand and assure her that things would get better.

He knew from experience. How many troubles had weighed on him? Wrestling with the issues, he had pulled himself up and moved forward, praying for a brighter day ahead.

Before she responded, the waiter arrived to take their order. When he left, Ian took a long drink of ice water, wetting his dry mouth before repeating his suggestion. "Why suffer alone?" He set his glass on the table, then sent her an understanding grin and tapped his shoulder. "Here's a place to cry if you need one."

Her gaze drifted to his arm, then rose. A gentle smile nudged her lips before she shook her head. "I shouldn't let it bother me. The problem is my sister's, not mine."

Without saying more, she fingered the water glass before raising it to her lips.

Ian's mind drifted back to the day he'd seen Esther and her sister at Bay Breeze. He'd wondered then if perhaps he'd interrupted a serious conversation. Women naturally opened up to other women...not men. Yet looking at her, Ian longed to relieve her tension and encourage the warm smile to stay instead of fading so fast.

"Family problems are natural," he said. "No way to get around them."

Esther nodded, knowing Ian was correct, but how could she tell him the whole story? She ran her hand along the length of her hair, wondering how to dig herself out of the mess she'd created.

"You're right," she said.

"We can talk about it," he offered again.

A gentle concern settled on his face, and she wanted to tell him…to tell someone how frustrated her father had left her after their talk, but she couldn't. "Why ruin a friendly lunch?"

He shrugged, looking puzzled. Seeing his face, Esther realized she owed him some kind of explanation.

Silence hung in the air.

"I tried to talk to my father…for my sister," Esther said finally, "but sometimes he uses the Scriptures for his own purpose."

"You're struggling with the commandments? Like how do you honor your father and not agree with him?"

"That, too, I suppose." His comment, truer than he realized, surprised her. "No, it's more bizarre than that." She cringed when she finished the sentence. Could she ever keep her mouth shut?

"Not sacrificing the firstborn, I hope." A grin spread across his face.

"No, that would be me. Nothing that dire."

"Glad to hear there'll be no bloodshed."

The silence returned, and Esther struggled to give him a sensible response before letting it drop. "My sister and Jeff want to get married. That's all."

"Ah, your dad doesn't like Jeff? It happens all the time."

Agreeing with his explanation settled in Esther's thoughts, but she couldn't lie to him. "No, my dad likes him very much."

Ian shook his head, a puzzled scowl etched on his face. "I don't get it."

"Neither do Rachel and I. Dad thinks—" she

swallowed the full story "—she's too young to marry. I'd hoped to convince him otherwise, but I failed."

"Too young? You're kidding. How old is she?"

"Twenty-six."

For a moment his frown deepened, then it shifted to reassurance. "Sounds like you did your best."

Her best? Guilt stabbed her. "Maybe not my best, but I tried," she conceded.

She'd failed in many ways, disappointing her father and letting Rachel down again. Her sister gave her more credit than she deserved. Not only had the conversation with her father been useless, but it seemed to drive the concept more firmly into his stubborn mind.

Being the firstborn and raised under her father's strict thumb, Esther found herself unable to stand up to his ways. For so long she had striven for perfection to please him. Yet she'd never succeeded. She had no idea how to make her father happy...other than finding a husband.

Rachel reacted in her own way. She responded to their father's rules with the proverbial "grain of salt" and often prodded him to change his mind. Esther couldn't do that. Still, for Esther and her sister, God's word about honoring parents always won out, no matter how unreasonable her father could be.

Esther pushed the thoughts from her mind. Instead of moping, she needed to change the subject. She opened her mouth to ask about his research, but Ian looked past her and gestured to the waiter who had appeared behind her. The server slid Ian's mile-high sandwich in front of him, then set her bowl of soup on the table.

When he had gone, Esther dipped the spoon into the wide noodles and hunks of chicken, using the time to get her thoughts in order. With her first bite, the savory broth sent a soothing warmth through her. Thinking of Ian's words about "good for what ails you," she grinned and watched him concentrate on his sandwich.

If she ever were to fall in love, she'd choose a man like Ian. His gentle good nature seemed as calming as the chicken soup...except she sometimes felt rattled by the unfamiliar feelings that came over her in his presence and seemed unable to hold an intelligent conversation.

Swallowing a few more spoonfuls, Esther pushed the bowl aside.

When Ian looked up from his triple-decker, he chuckled. "I should have ordered the soup. I'm ready to burst."

Not wanting the conversation to tread where it had been, she sent it in a new direction. "So tell me about the research." She leaned against the seat bench. "What type of information are you looking for?"

"The mast, for one thing," he said. "I need to replace the original one, and I'm weighing the choices. Solid wood—Sitka spruce or Douglas fir. Or possibly laminated. That's less expensive, but then I need to worry about the glue. Maybe aluminum. I'm not sure what I want. Then I'm considering upgrading the furling system."

"Can't help you there," she said, "but I'm sure we can find some information at the library."

"I figured you'd know where to look." He pushed his index finger against the center of his spectacles and looked at her as if he had something else to say...but he didn't.

"Thanks for the company. I'd better get back to work," Esther said, opening her wallet and drawing out some bills.

"Let me buy you lunch," Ian said. "It's the least I can do."

Though she shook her head, he insisted and nabbed the bill from the table before she did. He strode ahead of her to the cash register, and she decided not to embarrass him by arguing.

Outside as they headed back to the library, Esther noticed the casual way he ambled beside her. A gentle breeze blew and ruffled strands of dark hair against his forehead. He lifted his fingers and drew them through his locks, adjusted his glasses by the earpiece and gave her a smile.

Amazed, Esther felt a flutter in her chest. She drew her hand upward against the decorative patch on her denim dress to contain the alien feeling.

"I'll take my vacation time next week, spending it at the city marina," Ian said, seemingly unaware of the tremor beneath her hand. "I'd like you to stop by and see the work I'm doing on the boat...and I'd like to hear what you think about it."

"Sailboats and I don't mix," she said, flinging out the comment to cover her discomfort. "I haven't sailed in years...not since—"

"I know," he said, "but you ride in cars, and they're much more dangerous."

He was right, but that didn't make the memories any easier. The experience that horrible day had changed her life. Looking into his smiling eyes, she wanted to toss away her fears, but they involved more than sailing. Esther had set her mind on a single life. Unable to open her heart to hurt and rejection, Esther refused to get excited over a little masculine attention.

Besides, from her experience, men were fickle. With the speed of light they seemed to lose interest in hobbies, possessions and even friendships. Her library patrons attested to that. Women remained faithful to their favorite authors and genres. Men's interests seemed to wander.

Esther shook her head. "I can't make any promises."

"None required," he said. "I'll be there every day until dark. I could show you the boat and...we could have dinner."

"I have the research business," she said. "That doesn't leave much time."

She watched his smile fade, and her own joy dimmed. If only she could say yes, but she didn't have any interest in romance...not even a platonic male friend. The whole idea lent itself to trouble.

"If you change your mind, you're welcome to drop by any time," he said as they climbed the steps to the library.

"Thanks," she said, wanting to end the conversation. She followed him through the front door and headed for the back to remove her jacket and stow her shoulder bag.

When she returned, she saw he'd found his way to the computers where several patrons searched for information. Instead of offering help, Esther strode to the desk and tried to forget his invitation, which hung before her like a carrot.

She'd become independent and solitary for too long. Against her better judgment she let her gaze drift toward Ian. He stared at the computer screen, shaking his head in seeming frustration.

Nabbing her common sense, she faced the truth. A librarian assisted patrons. Without further hesitation she headed his way, certain that she could find what he needed more quickly than he could.

Now, if she could only do the same for herself.

Chapter Three

"Say that again," Rachel said, disbelieving her ears.

"Let's elope." Jeff grasped her hand and kissed her fingers. "That will solve our problem. Run away and get married. People do it all the time."

"Not this people." Rachel gazed at him, amazed at his suggestion. "You know how I was raised, Jeff. I couldn't do that to my dad or Esther."

"We'll ask your dad's forgiveness after it's over. And Esther—she's a problem. We'll never have a wedding if we're waiting for her. Let's elope, Rachel. That's our only solution."

Since the day Esther had told her that once again she'd made no headway with their father, Rachel had seen no hope. Tears blurred her vision and rolled down her cheeks. She loved Jeff, and no doubt he loved her, but she had been raised knowing God expected her to obey her parents. The Lord commanded it, and Rachel could do nothing else—no matter how much she loved Jeff. "I can't," she whispered.

"Then what can we do?" He released her hand and fell against the sofa cushion. "This doesn't make sense, Rachel. You know it and I know it. I'm sorry. Waiting is hopeless. We have to do something."

"Like what?" she said, trying to be brave while with her sleeve she mopped the tears that dripped from her chin.

"We need to get Esther in gear. Find her a husband."

Rachel's heart yo-yoed to her toes and back. "What? Do you hear what you're saying?"

"What else is there? I want to marry you before we're too old to enjoy it." He slammed his fist against his leg. "Think. If Esther stays single the rest of her life, we'll have to wait until she dies. Is that stupid, or what?"

"Don't say things like that. You're being unreasonable." Her heart rose to her throat. He hadn't been unreasonable. Her father was, and Jeff had been accurate. Unless Esther married or her father had a change of heart—and that seemed inconceivable—Rachel would be single the rest of her life.

Jeff glowered at her, his cheeks flushed. "You think I'm being unreasonable?"

Rachel captured his hands and cupped them in hers. "I'm sorry, Jeff. You're not at all unreasonable. You've been more patient than any man I know. We'll think of something."

"Look, why can't we give it a try? Your birthday is two weekends away. I planned to give you a little party…so why not include two or three single guys from the resort? We'll make sure Esther's there.''

He beamed, and Rachel hated to dim his plans. ''Most single men date. Won't they bring someone along?''

His smile faded, as she had expected. ''Okay. How about Hal? He's single and lives in the next apartment…and he isn't dating. I'll tell him about the good-looking single woman who'll be at the party.''

''Would he come?'' Even if he did, Rachel knew her sister. Esther would be standoffish and scowl through the whole party if she had any idea they were trying to play matchmaker. ''It won't work. I know it.''

''Have faith, Rachel. Bay Breeze has the big Fourth of July party. I'll see to it that Esther gets an invitation…somehow.'' He dragged his fingers through his boyish blond hair. ''We can at least give it a try.''

His sweet, pleading grin sent her heart galloping. How could she say no? He'd already said it. This could be her only chance at marrying Jeff. Even though he loved her, how much longer would he wait?

''Okay,'' she said, ''we'll give it a try. But promise no one will be hurt…especially Esther.''

''Promise.'' He slid his arm across her shoulders and drew her closer. ''I love you,'' he whispered in her ear. She yielded her lips to his, praying that God would guide their actions. If she hurt Esther, she'd never forgive herself…or Jeff.

* * *

Esther slowed her steps, astounded that she had prodded herself to visit the bustling marina. She'd waited two weeks before accepting his invitation. While some boats stood in dry dock for maintenance or repair, others hummed into the slips with well-tuned motors, their sails furled.

Embarrassed, she stood on the pier and eyed the many boats, wondering which one belonged to Ian. She'd never asked the name—and now she stared at *Suzie II, Bright Penny, Just 4 Fun,* a multitude of catchy phrases. While she studied the boats to find Ian, her stomach turned cartwheels. Why had she come?

As she turned away to escape the busy pier, a voice sailed through the breeze.

"Esther?"

Pivoting, she scanned the dock again and, seeing him, sent Ian an uneasy wave as he bounded toward her.

"I'm glad you came," he said, a shy smile playing on his lips. "I'd nearly given up hope that you'd take me up on my offer."

She'd thought the same. Still, seeing his pleased look gave her a warm feeling. "I had the day off and decided it was too lovely to sit inside doing research."

"I'm glad," he said. "Come see what I've done...with help. I decided I couldn't do it alone." He beckoned her to follow.

Walking behind him, Esther admired his build. In the library and at the resort, his physique had often been hidden beneath a suit jacket or windbreaker.

Today, a T-shirt snuggled against his well-toned chest. His tanned arms rippled with muscles. He seemed like a seaman…as Uncle Jim had looked while raising the sails or fighting a bullying wind.

The memory squeezed against her heart, but Ian's enthusiasm drew her forward.

"Can you climb?" he asked, pointing to the ladder.

She nodded, glad that she'd worn sneakers and a pair of jeans. He waited behind her as she moved up the ladder, and at the top he hovered nearby to give her a boost onto the boat deck, then followed.

"What's her name?" Esther asked, straightening her back and eyeing the freshly polished hull.

Ian ran his hand along the railing feeling the smooth, polished wood. "She's called *Lady Day*," he said, "but captains always want to rename their boat. I'll give her a new name when I christen her."

She nodded and looked toward the horizon, drawing in a breath of air drifting up from the river and the connecting lake. Ian stood so near she caught the fragrance of his sun-warmed skin and the faint scent of spicy citrus.

"What do you think? Good progress, huh?"

She had no idea what work went into refurbishing a sailboat, but she recalled her uncle's sloop and thought the cutter looked in good shape. "It looks great. What's left to do?"

"Install the mast, repair the mainsail and finish the painting. Another week and it'll be finished. That gives me more than a week to sail her and see how she does."

The thought set her on edge, but she hid her discomfort. "I'm sure it'll be great."

"How about coming along? I'll have her out a couple days first. We could take her out a week from Saturday. What do you say?"

She lowered her eyes, wishing with all her heart she could say yes. She remembered the wonderful feeling of being out on the water, the wind in her hair, the sun warming her skin. "You know how I feel, Ian. Anyway, my sister's birthday party is that day."

"Oh," he said, with disappointment echoing in his voice.

"I'm sorry, Ian." To her surprise, Esther meant it.

Perspiration rolled down his face, and he pulled off his spectacles and wiped moisture from the bridge of his nose with his handkerchief.

Esther fixed her gaze on his handsome face, usually hidden behind the heavy glasses. His sculpted nose looked unburdened and the deep blue of his eyes shone with more brilliance.

He grinned, and two dimples winked at her before he slid the glasses back on. "One day I'm getting contacts. I hate these things…especially in summer."

"You look good without those heavy frames hiding your face," Esther said before she could harness her words. "I'm sorry. That sounded rude. You're nice looking with them, too." No matter what she said she dug herself in deeper. She'd become tactless when it came to social conversation. Life seemed easier in the library, where she felt comfortable and competent with her work.

"Listen," he continued, as if he hadn't heard what she'd said, "how about Sunday? You usually don't work on Sunday." He searched her eyes. "Right?"

She nodded.

"I'd really like to show you how safe sailing can be." His eyes pleaded with her.

"I promise," he continued, "we'll stay close to shore, and at any sign of clouds I'll bring you right back to port. Now, there's an offer you can't refuse."

His plaintive tone made her laugh. "Maybe sometime...when you put it that way." She hesitated, wondering why she had even thought about saying yes. A prayer shuffled through her, asking God for direction. "Let me think about it, okay?"

"Okay. That's better than no."

His look melted her heart, but she tempered her desire to change her mind and accept his invitation. "You've done a nice job with the cutter. I'm sure you'll enjoy sailing her."

He nodded, but his look left her feeling responsible for his gloom.

"How about lunch?" he asked.

"Only if I pay."

His face paled, then he recovered. "Is that the only way you'll have lunch with me?" A boyish smile inched across his face.

"That's right," she said, feeling herself weaken with each plea.

"Okay. This time," he said finally.

This time. The words hung in the air, then slithered down her spine like ice water. What was she doing? She'd spent the past ten years accepting her single life. Ian was prying at her conviction with every gentle smile.

She needed to protect herself. She needed to stay away from Ian.

Ian closed Philip Somerville's door and headed for his office. His head ached, and he wondered why the owner of Bay Breeze had asked him to research the possibility of adding a fleet of charter boats to the resort.

Thinking back, he recalled that Philip had asked him to do research once before—investigate local resorts to identify the amenities they offered. At the time, he'd felt as if Philip were trying to play matchmaker, pushing him and Jemma Dupre together. To his utter embarrassment, Jemma had rejected him from the word go and soon after, to many people's surprise, she'd become Philip's wife. Yet despite their age difference—the crux of Philip's problem—they appeared to be a happy and well-suited couple.

Facing his new assignment, Ian knew he might have jumped at the research job three weeks earlier. Then he'd known exactly where he could go for help…but since Esther had declined his boating invitation with more than a cold shoulder, he hesitated to ask for her service.

Her service. That was it. If Esther wanted to run a research business, she should be willing to work with him on this project. She couldn't turn down business. Or could she?

He pressed his finger between his eyes to soothe his headache. Jarring his frames, he pulled off his glasses and eyed them. Esther's voice sailed into his thoughts. *You look good without those heavy frames hiding your face.* He hadn't responded, but he knew she was right. He'd been saying it for years. He needed contacts. Sliding on his spectacles, he hurried into his office and made a note to himself. Call the optometrist.

Dropping the memo pad onto the desk, he sank into his chair and thought about Esther. What had created the distance he sensed when he spoke to her? Sailing? She'd made it clear she didn't sail. But he'd hoped to change her mind—show her what pleasure she could have if the captain used common sense.

Common sense? If he had any, he'd find someone else to do the research for him. He rose, crossed the room and lifted the yellow pages from a bookshelf, deciding he'd use his head and find another research company.

Back at his desk, he opened the cover and slid his finger along the index. Research. Laboratories See Chemists...no. He moved his finger down the list. Economic Research and Analysis. Educational Research. Information Search and Retrieval. Could that be it?

He found the page and skimmed the listings. He grazed past the businesses until his focus fell on Esther Downing Research Services. He closed his eyes, his pride rearing in his head. Could he bear another rejection?

Closing the phone book, Ian pulled her business card from his wallet and gazed at the number. He knew she would still be at the library. Should he leave a message on her answering machine? That seemed safest. If she returned his call, the choice would be hers.

He punched in the number and waited as it rang. Hearing the click, he listened for her message.

"Esther Downing Research Services. May I help you?"

He felt his jaw drop, and he caught his breath. "Esther?"

"Yes," she said, the word fading. Did she recognize his voice?

"This is Ian. I thought I'd get your machine." He rubbed the nape of his neck to relieve the fresh tension.

"Ian...I thought it was you."

The line was weighted with silence.

"I'm off today," she said finally.

Business call, Ian reminded himself. "I wondered if you'd have time for a research project. Philip Somerville, who owns Bay Breeze, asked me to study the possibility of buying or contracting a fleet of charter boats for the resort."

Silence.

Ian cleared his throat. "I need advice. Someone who knows the right questions to ask and where to find the answers. I thought of you...naturally."

A sigh fluttered over the line. "I'm working on a big project at the moment. When do you need the information?"

When? Philip hadn't mentioned a time line. Ian closed his eyes and thought. "I don't suppose he's expecting a completed project this tourist season. When will you be available?"

Papers rustled over the wire and he waited. "Next week, I suppose," she said. "If that won't work, I can refer you to another research service."

"No," Ian said, nearly cutting her off, "a week is fine. Should we set up an appointment?" Appointment. The word sounded cold and unfriendly.

"How about a week from Tuesday? Evening. Let's say seven o'clock." Her voice was charged with business.

"Seven's fine. Thanks." What could he do to soften her tone...to bring back the Esther he'd admired for the past year? More than admired, if he faced the truth. "By the way, did you enjoy the birthday party?"

Silence.

"You mean Rachel's?"

"Right," he said. "I hope you had a nice time."

Esther closed her eyes and fumbled for a response. She'd had a horrible time. Her sister's ploy had been obvious. Or had it been Jeff's idea? The evening tumbled through her thoughts. "It was okay," she said. "Nothing to write home about."

"Family birthdays are like that sometimes, I suppose."

Another lengthy pause caused her discomfort, and Esther wished he'd say something or say goodbye. Tension knotted in her neck and coiled around her shoulder blades.

"A week from Tuesday, then," he repeated. "At seven."

"Right."

"Is your address correct in the telephone book?"

"Yes, and please use the side door. That's my office." Her voice sounded hard and unnatural in her ears.

"Right." He hesitated again. "I'll see you then."

The telephone clicked and died, but remembrance of his voice saying her name sailed through her head like a kite on the wind, dipping and soaring, taking her breath away. Foolish.

Men. She didn't need the hassle. She thought of Rachel's birthday party. Poor Hal. His face loomed in her thoughts. No doubt her sister or Jeff had set her up. The intent seemed obvious. Scrape the barrel and find poor Esther a man.

Shame dragged at her heart. Hal had done everything he could to show interest in her. He'd brought her a drink and sat beside her telling the mundane story of his life…though hers had been no better…while she wallowed in misery. Couldn't people just accept that she wanted to be single?

And why had she agreed to handle the Bay Breeze job? She could easily have told Ian it would be a month, maybe two, before she'd be free. As often as logic warned her to steer clear of him, her heart led her in the opposite direction. Asking for trouble, that's what she was doing.

Her father came to mind. If faith could move mountains, then faith could guide her. Years ago she'd felt God's call to be on her own. God? Or had it been her own decision? No matter, she felt ready to let God be in control.

An unexpected grin tugged at her lips. She'd *try* to let God be in control. She preferred to hold the reins.

Chapter Four

Esther stared at the invitation before dropping it to her desk. Another of her sister's ploys. Annoyance rifled through her. Why would she receive an invitation to the Bay Breeze Fourth of July celebration unless Rachel had manipulated it? Esther reconsidered. No. Not Rachel. Never. The perpetrator had to be Jeff.

Running her index finger around the edge of the attractive card, Esther closed her eyes. Should she be angry or laugh at the charade? Hadn't Rachel and Jeff realized their previous matchmaking attempt had failed miserably? Then again she couldn't blame them.

She flipped aside the white-and-gold card with her thumb and finger, dismissing the invitation that reminded her she was ruining Rachel's life. She eyed her watch. No time for feeling bad about it now. Ian would be arriving any minute.

She'd tried to anticipate his questions ahead of

time so their meeting could be brief. Brief? Loneliness washed over her. Lately she missed him. He hadn't dropped by the library since she'd refused the Sunday boat trip a few weeks ago. Had she been foolish? What could be wrong with developing a friendship?

Friendships were something Esther didn't have. Sure, she had co-workers and acquaintances, but friends? They didn't seem to fit into her life…or was it that she didn't fit into theirs?

She found Ian amiable and interesting—even attractive—but…a friendship could lead to more than she wanted. And being friends with a man who sailed? Why drag her fears out in public?

But that was foolish. Ian had offered her every safety precaution—sailing close to the shore and docking at the first sight of a cloud. What danger would there have been? None…except for her jangling emotions when she saw him.

The doorbell sounded and jerked Esther to attention. She drew in a lengthy breath, then rose and headed for the door. She could see Ian through the windowpane, his dark wavy hair tousled in the breeze.

Ignoring her charging pulse, she swung open the door. "Come in." Her arm directed the way. "Have a seat."

An uneasy look flashed across his face as he stepped past her and strode into her small office. Inside, he stood midfloor.

"Please have a seat," she repeated. "I'll work at the desk so I can take notes."

He did as she asked and laid a notepad on the small table beside the armchair.

Feeling uncomfortable herself, Esther stood a moment, questioning her behavior. Ian was a client, and she should treat him as kindly as anyone who came to the door for her services. She recaptured her graciousness. "Would you like some coffee? Or tea?"

"Coffee sounds good," Ian said, a hesitant look on his face. "Thanks."

She turned and strode through the doorway and across the landing to her compact kitchen. Earlier she'd anticipated his preference, and with the pot ready to go, Esther punched the button on the coffeemaker with satisfaction. While the coffee circulated through the brewer, she pulled cups from the cabinet, then paused, pinching the bridge of her nose while she anticipated her next move.

Esther rarely made cookies. So why had she done so after work tonight? Because a man's heart is through his stomach? Hogwash. She'd wanted a treat. That was her reasoning…and she was sticking to it.

Opening the cookie jar, she selected a few cookies and arranged them on a plate. Irritation riffled up her back. If she could only control her wavering emotions. She calmed herself as she poured the brew into the cups, and after she placed everything on a tray, she returned to her office.

"I could smell you before you came through the doorway," Ian said. He hesitated, his expression wavering. "I mean…the coffee. I could smell the coffee. Not you."

His discomfort caused her to laugh. "I realized you meant the coffee." She set the tray on the desk and handed him a cup and napkin, adding the option of milk or sugar. He declined.

"Would you like a cookie?" She extended the plate. "Homemade." She cringed, hearing her Betty Homemaker pride.

"They look good," he said, and slid one from the plate. "I'm partial to peanut butter."

"Take two...or three." She shoved the plate toward him for encouragement.

He picked up a couple more and placed them on the napkin. "Thanks. I don't get homemade often."

"Same here," she said, and wished she hadn't.

Sliding into her desk chair, Esther focused on her drink. Silence hung between them as they sipped the coffee and bit into the sweets. Esther wrestled with what to say next. Should she ask about sailing? Maybe sticking to business would be less stressful. The unwelcome feeling of loneliness washed over her as she weighed her options.

"Did you enjoy sailing?" she asked finally. "How was that first weekend?"

His head moved at a snail's pace to meet her gaze while a look of surprised pleasure settled on his face. "It was great. Thanks." His shoulders relaxed, and he leaned forward, resting an arm on his knee, a half-eaten cookie dangling from his fingers. "You should have been there. She handles like a dream. I have to thank you for your help."

She shook her head. "I only showed you where to

find the books. You did the research and worked the miracle.''

A faint grin curved his mouth. ''It was a miracle of sorts. That poor lady was in bad shape. I didn't know how bad until I got inside, but she looks great now.''

''Yes. She did when I saw her,'' Esther said. ''Just be…careful when you're out there. Keep an eye and ear on the weather.'' She swallowed her mothering thoughts. ''You know…''

''I do know.'' He set his cup on the table and brushed cookie crumbs from his fingers. ''My dad and I sailed years ago. He taught me everything I know about sailing. Not only the skill—he pounded a lot of his insight into my head. Wisdom and caution when it comes to sailing.'' He gave her a warm smile. ''Each time I sail I hope to honor him.''

''Honor your father and mother,'' Esther said. Hearing her voice surprised her. She cleared her throat and ran her fingers across the back of her neck. ''I suppose we should get started.''

''Good idea,'' Ian said, but his look let her know he suspected her comment had a deeper meaning.

She moved her mug aside and pulled forward a manila folder. Inside she'd made her notes, anticipating his needs. ''Now…where should we begin?'' When she lifted her eyes from the paper, she noticed his faint grin.

''I always think the beginning is good.''

His fleeting smile sent her heartbeat skipping for a moment. ''You're right.'' Quieting her pulse, she took a minute to scan the information. ''First, we need to compile a list of all aspects involved in owning excursion boats. Purchase price, storage and maintenance, crew costs.'' She lifted her gaze. ''Their wages and benefits.''

Ian nodded, shifting his chair closer to eye her notepad. ''Insurance.''

''Yes, definitely.'' She jotted down his point. ''We need to talk with dealers…but even more, we'll want to speak with some charter companies. They'll have the tried-and-true info.'' She lifted her head from the notes.

''Right. The real lowdown,'' Ian agreed.

Esther tapped her pencil. ''Do you think Mr. Somerville is interested in fishing boats? Or just excursions?''

Ian shrugged. ''I'll have to get more from him on that. He owns a sailboat, so I think he has sailing in mind. You know…a sunny afternoon on the lake. But my guess is fishing charters would bring new business. That's not a bad idea.''

''I'll look at both, then. I've made a list of some of the charter fishing and excursion companies in the area.'' She massaged the middle of her forehead a moment, realizing the research job would be time-consuming. Maybe more time than she wanted to spare.

''Is something wrong?'' Ian's concerned voice caught her off guard.

''No…well…I just realized this is a big project. I'm not sure I have the time to do a thorough job.'' She dropped the pencil on the notepad and leaned back in the chair, wanting to laugh at herself. What else did she do with her time? Cleaning her dresser drawers and kitchen cabinets took only so long. Then she thought of reading—one of her favorite solitary activities.

Solitary. That was her life, it seemed. She eyed Ian watching her from his chair. Flustered by his attentiveness, she bent over the desk and grasped the pencil. Having nothing to write, she twirled it between her fingers. Though she was uncomfortable, having a man look at her with admiration felt good.

Ian's expression shifted through a kaleidoscope of emotions before he rose and rested his palms on the front of her desk. "I'm confident in you, Esther. Are you thinking you're not capable of this job? I know you are."

"It's not my capability," she said, wondering what was going through his mind. "It's the number of hours it will take." *Face it.* Her concern wrapped around spending time with Ian.

"Don't worry about the cost. Somerville can afford it. And he'll pay you well." He straightened his back.

"It's not the money. It's—" She studied the wood grain on her desktop, afraid to look in his eyes. "Me."

Her head jerked upward, a scowl tugging at her brow. "You?"

Defensiveness settled on his tense face. "Ever since I asked you to go sailing, I've sensed—"

Aware of her behavior, Esther looked away and took a shuddered breath. She scared people away with her unyielding personality. "It's not you, Ian."

She paused, knowing that part of it was him. Still, that wasn't fair to him. He'd done nothing. Nothing at all...except love sailing and, unknowingly, rattle her emotions. "I'm thinking about the amount of time I have to work on a project this large. I work full-time at the library. Remember?"

He circled the desk and stood at her side, resting his hand on her chair back. "I know it'll take time. Just give me something to offer Somerville. A cost estimate and time factor, and I'll talk it over with him. If he has any qualms, then I'll look somewhere else."

He slid off his spectacles and rubbed the bridge of his nose. His intense gaze didn't waver from her face.

Weighing her decision, Esther waited a moment to speak. "I charge forty dollars an hour, but I'll have to give the time frame some thought."

"That's fair enough." He slid on his glasses.

Surprising her, he leaned across her desk and fingered her Bay Breeze invitation. "Fourth of July?"

Afraid of what he'd see if he looked into her eyes, Esther focused on the card and nodded.

"It's a good party," Ian said. "I'm usually there...half working, half enjoying myself."

"Half working?"

"I'm expected to keep things running smoothly for Somerville. Greet guests. Make sure everyone's having a good time." He stepped back and shrugged. "This is a public relations event as much as a celebration. City council, mayor, business people. You get the picture."

Swiveling in her chair, she faced him squarely.

"Do you have any idea why I'd be invited? It doesn't make any sense."

Ian's mouth opened, then closed without a word. He rounded her desk and picked up the invitation. "Why not?" he asked finally.

She knew why not. The invitation had been arranged by Jeff. Frustrated, Esther rose. "It doesn't matter," she said, wondering why in the world she'd asked him the question.

"For whatever reason," Ian said, sinking into his chair, "come along. You'll have a good time. Seeing the fireworks from the penthouse is a treat."

Treat or not, Esther had no plans to be there.

Returning to his chair, Ian lifted the coffee cup.

Certain it was empty, Esther rose. "Let me refresh that for you."

As she extended her arm toward the cup, Ian caught her hand. "I'm sorry about what I said earlier, Esther."

She knew what he meant, but she didn't want to talk about the sailing invitation. "No problem," she said, grasping the cup and turning toward the doorway.

Ian watched her go and waited. Obviously she wanted to avoid the topic, but he needed to get things out in the open. He liked Esther. He'd always liked her...the way she smiled, the way she talked with people, the way she loved books. Now, when he'd finally made a little progress, she'd slipped through his fingers like an errant ice cube escaping the freezer tray.

He'd often thought about those little cubes plotting

amongst themselves. He could almost hear them whispering. "Wait until he opens the freezer door. When he goes for one of us, you jump." The image brought a foolish grin to his face, and before he could contain it, Esther came through the doorway.

"Something funny?" she asked, crossing to him with the filled mug.

She hadn't gotten a fresh cup for herself, and he eyed hers sitting on the desk. "I was thinking about ice cubes."

She stopped and drew back. "Ice cubes?"

"It's a long story."

"Really?" She tilted her head, an amused look growing on her lips. "I'd like to hear it."

He eyed her empty cup. "Only if you let me freshen your drink." He rose and snatched her coffee mug from the desk, ignoring her startled expression. Before she could respond, he swept past her toward the doorway he assumed led to the kitchen.

He barreled through the doorway, finding himself in a compact galley as neat and organized as Esther's library. Heading for the brewer, he snatched a cookie from the jar while noting her spice rack, each container lined up in alphabetical order. He suspected she cataloged her canned goods in the same way.

After filling the mug, he returned and found Esther standing in the same spot he'd left her. He set the coffee on the small table beside his seat and rounded her desk for her office chair. Rolling it to the table, he beckoned to her. "Sit in the armchair. I'll use this." Before she could argue, he slid onto the one she'd used earlier.

Dumbfounded, she sat.

He took a sip of the fresh brew. "Let's forget the ice cubes and—"

Esther shook her head. "No way."

He went ahead and told her his foolish notion about the ice cubes' antics.

A smile blossomed on her face and a laugh bubbled from her chest. "I've had the same thought. I figured I was the only weirdo to think something that warped."

Her laugh sounded wonderful, and he watched her shoulders relax. She lifted the mug and took a sip. "I have more cookies."

"I sneaked one while I was in the kitchen," he admitted.

"Good," she said. But her smile faded too soon and the tension he'd seen earlier reappeared.

He slumped against the chair back, sorry to see the stress return. Expecting silence, he pondered what to say next. Perhaps he should finalize their business and leave rather than create any more distance between them.

With his decision still unsettled, Esther took another sip of coffee before leaning against the armrest. "I owe you an apology."

Her words caught him by surprise. "You do?"

"You were right earlier when you said I'd acted differently since you invited me to sail. I'm sorry."

"No need, Esther. I understand your feelings. Maybe I was wrong to ask." He rolled the chair closer, his knees nearer hers.

She shook her head. "No, it's natural. If you love sailing, you want to share it with friends."

Friends. Did she really consider him a friend? Her wavering manner made him uneasy—creating distance rather than friendship. But he understood her attitude toward sailing. "I wish you could see your face when I talk about sailing. Somewhere underneath your apprehension, I sense a longing to sail again. I think under all those fears you miss it."

He caught her faint nod as if in agreement.

"Your face seemed to brighten the day you stood on the boat and we talked about sailing," Ian continued. "I guess I wanted to share the experience with you. Remember the sun and wind flapping the sails like it did years ago?"

"I'm being foolish," she said. "I wanted to accept. I've missed sailing, but anxiety hits me and I freeze. Give me time. Maybe one day I'll accept your offer."

He reached forward and caught her hand. "But only when you're ready. I'll try not to bug you. Promise."

Her gaze fell to his hand holding hers, and realizing what he'd done, Ian slipped his fingers away slowly for her sake, not his own. The feeling of her flesh against his—the warmth and softness of her touch—skittered through his veins, sending his pulse on a trot.

"Thanks," she whispered, her voice uncertain.

Fearing he'd pressed his luck, Ian shifted the chair away, enough to rise. "I suppose I'd better let you get back to work. Thanks for considering this project.''

"You're welcome," she said, rising and moving to his side.

"You can give me a call when you have the proposal ready." He pulled out his wallet and reached inside for a business card. "I'll let Somerville know you're working up something for him. A deal?" He handed her the card.

She accepted it with a nod. "A couple days. Okay?"

"Sure thing." He extended his hand, and Esther placed her smaller one in his. The same sensation accelerated his pulse again. He released her fingers and stepped back. "Thanks, Esther, and I hope to see you at the Fourth of July celebration."

"We'll see," she said.

He sensed she wouldn't come, but he wished she would. She would brighten the evening far more than the fireworks display. He knew that for sure.

Chapter Five

"What do you mean you're not going?" Rachel asked, her hands against her hips.

"Just what I said. You rigged the invitation. I'm not stupid."

Rachel marched across Esther's kitchen floor, frustration etched on her face. "Maybe you are stupid, Esther. I can't make Philip Somerville send you an invitation."

"No, but Jeff can. Or he bought Somerville's secretary a box of chocolates and she just happened to drop an invitation addressed to me in the mail." Watching her sister's face, Esther sensed she had neared the truth.

"It's a great party. I went last year." Rachel slid her arm across her sister's shoulder. "Please come. It'll be fun."

Tears filled Rachel's eyes, and Esther sank into despair. What could she do? If she didn't go, Rachel would be hurt. If she went, she would cause herself untold grief, avoiding the men Jeff had conspired with to do him a favor. It didn't make sense. They couldn't force someone to fall in love with her...or her with him. "I don't see the urgency. What difference does it make if I go or not?" Esther knew the difference, but she played dumb.

"I'm tired of seeing you lead the life of a recluse. You can at least get out and have fun."

Esther slid away from her sister's embrace and rested a hand on her shoulder. "What's fun for you isn't necessarily fun for me. Do you understand?"

"Yes, but—"

"Look," Esther said, trying to deal with her own frustration, "I'll think about it. That's all I can promise."

"Thank you. I'm just worried about you." Rachel adjusted her shoulder bag and stepped back.

Esther felt her defenses slip away. Her heart softened, seeing her sister's desperation. "You should talk with Dad again. I know it seems useless, but..." Her words faded as she regarded Rachel's defeated expression.

Rachel gave a faint shrug and headed for the side door. "I'll talk with you later." She lifted her hand in farewell as she pushed open the screen door and vanished.

Esther breathed a sigh and sank into a kitchen chair. She understood her sister's desperation, but it wasn't fair. Burying her face in her hands, Esther allowed her frustration to surface as tears, and when she'd calmed herself, she turned to the Lord. *Why me, God? Did You lead me to be single or did my*

*own fear of rejection and my inexperience cause me
to think it was You?*

No answer came to her. She knew God responded
in His own time, not hers, but she hoped the Lord
understood her dismay and would give her a clear
answer.

Certainly she could change her mind about marriage, but dating and opening her heart would only
lead to hurt and even greater loneliness. She'd seen
and felt that too much in her life already.

She pushed herself away from the table, poured a
large glass of orange juice for energy and headed to
her office. The report lay on her desk, and she opened
the folder and pulled out Ian's business card. She
needed to tell him the proposal was ready.

Ian. His name billowed into her mind like satin
fabric. She tried to gather her thoughts of him, but
they slipped and slithered in their own direction—
untamed, undisciplined, yet shimmering.

The sensation startled her, and she lifted an unsteady finger to punch in his office telephone number.

Esther left the parking lot and followed the route
to the Bay Breeze registration desk. Ian had seemed
pleased to hear from her, and though he'd offered to
drop by later in the evening, she'd decided to get out
of the house and drop the project folder off at his
office instead.

"Ian Barry's office, please?" she asked the clerk.

"To the left and down the hall," he said.

She thanked him and followed his directions. In a

moment she came upon the offices and in a heartbeat
Ian met her at the door. Curious, she looked at him.

He chuckled. "Jim—the guy at the desk—buzzed
me." He motioned her inside.

"I wondered," she said, accepting his invitation.

The office looked like so many others—dark pan-
eling, a desk and two semicomfortable chairs in front
of the desk with a small table between. The credenza
seemed the only place that reflected a little of Ian.
Amid a stack of magazines and folders sat a model
sailboat. A photograph of an elderly gentleman stood
near the vessel. Not far from that, Esther spotted another photo of Ian, a bit younger, with a woman nestled at his side, their faces radiant. They stood beside
an autumn-hued bush, the leaves unidentifiable. The
picture aroused her curiosity and squeezed a little at
her heart.

"Have a seat," he said.

She sat and nodded toward the credenza. "Is that
your father?" she asked, forcing her gaze away from
the other photograph.

"It is. I suppose the sailboat gave it away." He
grinned, and his cheerful mood lifted hers. "He gave
me the sailboat when I was a boy and told me someday I'd have a real one of my own."

"You fulfilled the prophecy," she said, pulling her
attention from the credenza. She longed to ask about
the woman.

He didn't comment further. Instead, he eyed the
folder in her hand. "So what do you have for me?"

"It's all here. Cost and time frame. If all goes
well, I should have a fairly comprehensive report by

the first of the year.'' She searched his face, wondering if that was too long.

''That's better than I expected.'' He took the folder and flipped through the pages while she watched.

''I hope I'm not biting off too much,'' she added.

He glanced her way. ''Maybe I can help a little. I might be able to squeeze some time from the boss.''

''But I don't expect you to do my work. I know—''

''I might enjoy it. The more I learn about the business the more helpful I can be to Bay Breeze. Know what I mean?''

He wiggled his eyebrows in a silly way, making her laugh.

''I guess I do,'' she said.

He closed the folder and rose. ''I'll go over this tomorrow. Once I have a handle on it, I'll present it to Philip. It looks good, Esther.''

He dropped the file onto his desk, then turned to face her. ''Have you eaten?''

''Eaten?''

''Dinner. A while back you mentioned you'd enjoy seeing the sunset from our dining room. Why not take advantage of the evening?''

''Oh…but I planned to have something light when I get home.'' She'd planned nothing. In her rush to bring the proposal to Ian, she hadn't given thought to food.

''We have light entrées here.'' He closed the distance between them and extended his hand. ''I'd like to buy you dinner.''

"But—"

"But nothing. You've done a great job with the proposal, and this is my way to say thanks. You're making my job easier. You know…a happy boss is a happy employee."

Her "but" had been heading nowhere. Instead of disagreeing, she acquiesced. His smile put her at ease, and she followed him through the doorway, retracing her steps back to the lobby.

When they passed the registration desk, he gave the man he'd called Jim a wave and guided her toward the dining room.

Tonight the tables overflowed with patrons. Ian spoke briefly to the hostess, and she led them to a table, miraculously empty, near the front of the resort, overlooking Lake Michigan.

The sun hung low in the sky, where muted colors already tinged the horizon. Esther anticipated a glorious sunset. "You have pull for a good table, I see."

Ian hung his head with a boyish grin and chuckled. "That's about all the pull I have."

"That's enough. The sky looks amazing already."

He turned his attention from her to the sun-speckled water beginning to tint with pastel coral and lavender. "Pretty," he said, "but I like the view I have."

She felt heat slide up her neck and settle on her cheeks. "You shouldn't say that."

"Why not? I mean it." Surprised at his blatant compliment, Ian studied her face, wondering if he'd upset her again.

She picked up the menu and opened it, avoiding his eyes.

He wanted to kick himself for a moment. But when he looked again, she seemed to have dismissed his comment and concentrated on the food choices.

He glanced at the menu, knowing it by heart, and made a mental selection before his thoughts segued to the last time he'd seen Esther in the dining room.

Discomfort jigged through him when he recalled his ridiculous comments...telling her sister he had a library card and talking about the fish.

Esther looked at him from behind the menu. "Good choices. I can't decide between the salmon fillet and the Mexican chicken salad."

"They're both great." This time he didn't mention the salmon was fresh.

The waiter arrived, and when Esther made her selection, she chose the salad. He returned quickly with tall glasses of iced tea and a basket of warm rolls.

Before Ian could pass the basket, Esther's attention was diverted to the window. As he'd hoped, the setting sun had decided to perform an extravaganza.

"Look," she said, leaning forward, her chin resting on her hand.

"Talk about God's glory."

"Have you ever tried to imagine heaven?" Esther asked. "When I see a sunset or snow-capped mountains like the Rockies, I wonder how heaven can top it...but it does."

"Whatever heaven's like, my dad's enjoying it. I can picture him sailing on a perfect lake in perfect weather."

"My mom would be gardening."

He lifted his head. "Your mom's dead?"

"She died a few years ago. Mom loved flowers. All kinds. I feel sad...sort of nostalgic when I visit Dad and see those bedraggled flower beds. A few pitiful perennials that need separating and weeding."

"You don't have a green thumb?" Ian asked.

"I've never tried. I suppose I should go over sometime and work on those beds. It's finding the time, and now, if this project takes off, by the time it's over winter will be here."

"Maybe next year, then. Do it as a tribute to your mother."

"Like you," she said, looking more relaxed than he'd ever seen, "with your sailboat. Making your dad's dream for you come true. That's nice, Ian."

He'd never thought of it quite like that. It was nice. In the quiet, he turned back to the window, enjoying her company and admiring the deepening hues across the horizon. The colorful display reminded him of July Fourth fireworks. "Will I see you next Thursday?"

A frown settled on her face. "Thursday?"

"The celebration. Somerville's party."

"Oh...I'm not sure. If my sister has her way, I'll be there." An uneasy look replaced the frown.

Her sister? Then he remembered she'd be there with Jeff. "She's anxious for you to see the fireworks?"

"Not really," she said, her answer cryptic and weighty.

"Then...why?" He knew he shouldn't ask, but

Esther intrigued him. Her discomfort always cloaked her in silence, and he longed to know what troubled her so often.

A sigh rippled across Esther's shoulders. She lowered her eyes as if in thought, then focused on him. "It's a long story. One that would bore you, I'm sure."

"Like the ice cubes?"

His comment took a minute to settle in. When it did, she laughed. "No, that's not boring...just odd. My story is not only boring, but one that makes me uncomfortable."

He leaned forward and brushed her hand with a finger. "But now you've caught my interest."

Her intense gaze was direct. "Really? You want me to bare my soul?"

"Maybe it will help. Two heads are better than one, they say."

She laughed. "I've heard that, but I'm not sure it's true."

She fell silent again for a moment, then inched her head upward and captured him with her look. "My sister is playing matchmaker. I don't like it."

"Matchmaker? With who?"

"Me."

"With you." A jolt of concern zigzagged down his back. "You and who?"

"Anybody. She's determined to find her single sister a husband."

"But why? I don't understand." Anxiety shot through him. Why did Rachel want to marry off Esther?

"Long ago I felt called to remain single. Don't ask why. It's complex. A mixture of inner feelings, passing time and destiny. I'm happy with my work and my life. Why take chances on being miserable?"

Her words smacked him. Ian agreed that she liked her work. But she seemed so solitary. So alone. He'd had other dreams and hopes. She'd make a wonderful wife, he felt sure. He expanded his chest. "So if you want to be single, why is Rachel so determined otherwise?"

"Because of my father. My *stubborn* father."

Honor your father and mother. The words hit him between the eyes. He remembered her saying them not long ago. "I'm still in the dark."

"My father has always insisted I experience things first because I'm the oldest. I had to force myself to do so many things because Rachel wanted to do them. If I refused, my sister had to do without."

Ian felt his mouth drop open like a front loader, and he tightened his jaw to keep it hinged together. He couldn't believe her father insisted she marry before Rachel could. "You're not telling me that—"

"Yes, I am," Esther said. "If I stay single, my father won't approve of Rachel's marriage. It's Old Testament thinking, but he won't change."

"And you can't move him?"

"Faith moves mountains, but not my father. He's as staunch as Mount Everest. He won't budge."

Ian had a difficult time understanding how someone could cling to that belief in contemporary society. Then a question rushed through his head. Had her father twisted the Scriptures to manipulate the situation? If he wanted to see her married, her father might do just that.

In the business world, Ian had known many people who took the rules and bent them to their own needs. No reason why someone couldn't do the same with the Bible. He'd probably done it himself.

"Why not elope?" Ian asked as the impossibility struck him.

"How can we honor our father and go against his wishes?"

Stymied, Ian nodded. Looking at her expression, he knew Esther felt the same. The problem seemed insurmountable. "I don't have an answer. What I do know is you obviously can't fall in love at your sister's whim."

"You got it. Now, try to explain that to Rachel." As if captured by another new thought, her head snapped upward. "And it's not totally Rachel. I'm sure it's Jeff, too. He's tired of waiting. She can't even wear the ring he bought her...at least, not around Dad."

"You've got the dynamic duo plotting against you, and that's why you don't want to come to the party. I understand."

"Right, but I look at Rachel's tears, and..." Her voice faded as she brushed her finger across her eyes. "I don't have it in my heart to say no."

"Look, Esther." He paused, monitoring how he would tell her the plan generating in his mind. "I'll be there, and maybe I can help thwart Rachel's matchmaking."

"How can you do anything?" She leaned forward, her face a mixture of disbelief and hopefulness.

"If I'm hanging around you, the other guys will have the good sense to steer clear."

"But..."

The waiter's appearance halted her thought, and Ian took advantage of the situation. "Let's see how it goes. Okay? It might work."

With the waiter within earshot, Esther only nodded in agreement.

Ian dragged in a calming breath. Good fortune— maybe the Lord—had given him a prime opportunity. He bowed his head, thanking God for the food and for the unexpected opportunity.

Chapter Six

Esther stepped out of Jeff's car and looked up at the Bay Breeze penthouse. She'd never been inside the private rooms of the resort. As she followed Rachel and Jeff into the hotel, she realized she'd allowed that detail to pacify her objection to coming along. Being here at all sat heavily on her spirit.

No matter how she dealt with it, even Ian's offer to keep her company didn't make her happy about attending the Fourth of July celebration. Besides the matchmaking situation, she felt uncomfortable, knowing she really didn't belong with this group. She wasn't a politician, a big business exec, or a Bay Breeze employee. Her claim to fame was Jeff's desire to marry her sister. That was it.

Entering through the employees' entrance, Esther stood with her companions and waited for the private penthouse elevator. From her understanding, Philip Somerville lived in the rooms on the top floor of the resort.

The doors slid open and she stepped inside, catching a whiff of Rachel's perfume. Esther rarely wore a fragrance, but tonight she'd splashed on the one cologne she liked—a unique blend of flowers and herbs a library visitor had given her as a gift from the Isle of Capri.

Esther had been embarrassed that the woman had rewarded her for doing her job. All she'd done was pull together travel information about Italy for the woman. The subtle aroma drifted from Esther's warmed skin and made her think of palm trees, blue water and sun-kissed sand.

When the elevator doors opened, Esther stepped into an expansive terrazzo foyer. She was greeted by voices and laughter coming from a great room that lay ahead of her. Feeling terribly out of place, she edged behind Rachel as they entered the room.

Through an archway she spotted a formal dining room enticing people inside to investigate the trays of hors d'oeuvres and platters of desserts she could see in the distance. Stepping sideways, she hoped to vanish into the less occupied room, but before she escaped, Jeff dragged over the first prospect.

"Esther, this is Jim Mason. He works the registration desk."

Esther nodded. "Hi. I believe we've met."

For a heartbeat his face blanched with no obvious recognition, but Esther saved the day.

"I dropped by a few days ago to talk with Ian Barry. You buzzed him to say I was on my way down the hall."

"Right," he said, looking relieved. "I remember.

Yes.'' He moved closer to her side. ''I didn't know your name then. Now I do.''

''You do,'' Esther said, watching Rachel and Jeff glide away into the crowd, filled with hope. ''I was just heading in to look at the buffet.''

''May I get you a drink?'' he asked, moving along beside her. ''Wine or a cocktail?''

''Nothing alcoholic. Just a soft drink. Thanks,'' she said.

A curious look spread across his face. ''Okay, a soda it'll be.''

He scooted past her, heading for the beverage table beyond the overflowing dining-room table. Esther paused and eyed the fare. Shrimp, mushroom caps, ham roll-ups, pâtés, cheese, veggie tray, crackers, dips of all kinds. Not really hungry but needing something to distract her, she lifted a luncheon-size crystal plate and selected a sampling of appetizers.

When Jim reappeared, she accepted the drink, then stood beside him with both hands full, trying to figure out how she could juggle them to taste the snacks.

''Let's join the others,'' Jim said, beckoning her to follow.

If she'd had a choice, Esther would have dropped both items and dashed for the elevator, but she clung to one hope—Ian. He'd promised to save her. Esther hadn't seen him when she arrived, but thinking back, she realized she'd made a dash for the dining room without looking around.

Praying Ian was there somewhere, Esther followed Jim into the great room. Observing him with unbiased eyes, she admitted he was a clean-cut, nice-looking guy. Though she saw nothing wrong with him, she knew he'd been primed to get to know her better, and that in itself turned her into a warrior.

Guests mingled around the room—some standing in clusters, others seated in conversation areas, but Esther was intrigued by filtered sunlight spreading patterns on the beige carpet. She directed her gaze toward the French doors that opened to a wide balcony. As she neared, she could see fading sunlight spilling over the Lake Michigan horizon.

Though she preferred the quiet and less crowded second-floor terrace, she followed Jim, trying to balance her plate and drink as she maneuvered. He finally halted beside a small group of what she assumed were co-workers. As she tried to hold her drink while grasping a mushroom cap from her plate, a hand touched her shoulder, and her heart leaped when she turned and saw him.

"Hi. I've been looking for you," Ian said.

A sense of security flooded her, and she felt her tension ease. "I wondered where you were."

Jim drew back and eyed Ian, his face unsmiling. "I take it you two are friends," he said.

"That's right." Ian rested a hand on Esther's shoulder. "I'd like to borrow her if you don't mind." He sent Esther a comforting look.

"No problem," Jim said. A slight frown settled on his face.

"Philip Somerville wants to meet you. He's pleased with the proposal," Ian said, linking Esther's arm in his. "I told him you'd be here."

"You didn't," Esther said, her emotions giving way to disbelief. "Did he wonder why I was here?"

"He acted as if he knew," Ian said. Before moving away, he took Esther's drink from her. "Let's find a quiet spot, and I'll introduce you after you finish your plate."

She didn't care one iota about the food, but feeling protected, she drifted along behind Ian as he passed through the dining room and took a hallway to the right. At the first doorway he turned and she followed.

He'd led her to a study. Philip's, she assumed. The room had character—not leather and dark wood, but a brighter arrangement with windows looking over the resort's patio grill with flower gardens in the distance.

Royal-blue-and-beige-patterned upholstery looked homey and comfortable. She followed Ian's lead and sat on a matching chair, relieved to find a place to sit instead of balancing drink and plate. "It's hardly worth it," she said, gesturing to the food. "I only took it for something to do. My stomach's in knots."

Ian chuckled. "Eat up. It's good stuff. I think Jemma made some of it."

"Who's Jemma?"

"Philip's wife. She's a nice woman. A lot younger than he is. In fact…" He hesitated as if thinking better of it. "Someday I'll tell you a funny story about that."

A noise at the door caught their attention, and Esther followed Ian's gaze toward the doorway.

"Philip," Ian said, rising. He swung his hand toward Esther, motioning. "This is Esther Downing. You asked to meet her."

The good-looking man with salt-and-pepper hair extended his arm toward her in greeting, a warm smile on his face. "Nice to meet you, Esther. Thanks for coming."

"Thank you for…having me," she said. She'd stopped herself from saying "inviting me," since she still wasn't sure how she happened to be there.

"I don't know if Ian's told you, but I'm very impressed with your proposal," Philip said.

"Yes, he just mentioned it. Thank you, Mr. Somerville."

"Philip, please," he said. "I think you've covered all the bases, and I've answered some of your initial questions."

His compliment pleased her.

"Ian said he'd go over the points with you."

"That'll be fine," Esther said, feeling a nudge of eagerness. "I'm hoping I can keep the time line I set, but I'll try."

"That's all you can do." He nodded as if punctuating his statement, then turned to face Ian. "I see you found a quiet place to talk."

"Yes, sir, I hope you don't mind. Esther was balancing her plate and drink—"

"My house is yours, Ian." He hesitated, then chuckled. "Actually, my place will be somebody else's soon."

A frown sailed across Ian's face. "Come again."

"Jemma wants us to buy a house. And soon." He gave Ian a sly smile.

Ian's frown shifted to a look of pleasant surprise. "Anything you want to tell us?"

Philip eyed him with a sheepish grin. "We're announcing it before the fireworks tonight, but I'll let you in first on our secret. Jemma's expecting."

Ian's face brightened with genuine delight. "That's wonderful. Congratulations." He grasped Philip's hand and gave it a firm shake. "I'm really happy for you."

"Thanks. I never expected to be a father. Never in a million years. I think you know how much my life changed when Jemma came to town."

"I remember." A faint flush mottled his neck. "Very well."

Philip stepped to his desk and grasped a leather folder. "My calendar. You'd think these people would just enjoy the evening, but no. One of the city council members wants to make an appointment." He lifted his hand as he headed for the doorway. "Don't rush. It's nothing but noise out there."

With a smile he vanished around the corner, and Esther sat amazed at the dynamic gentleman she'd just met. "He's quite the man."

Ian nodded. "He is. He and his father turned a small hotel into this prosperous resort and made it look easy."

"His father's retired?" Esther asked.

"He died a few years ago. Philip inherited everything. His brother, Andrew, had opted out years earlier for a split of his share, to do his own thing. He hasn't been back that I know of. Even missed his father's funeral."

"There must be hard feelings or something," Esther said, wondering how anyone could miss his parent's funeral.

"He calls here once in a while. I think they've just grown distant." He stood and gestured toward the door. "Ready? I suppose we might as well let Rachel and Jeff see someone's taking care of you without their influence."

Esther grinned and rose, grabbing up her plate and glass.

When they passed through the dining room Ian took the dishes from her hand and set them on a sideboard before guiding her into the great room.

Esther's mind slid back to what he'd said earlier. Something about telling her a funny story about Philip's wife. She sensed it also had something to do with Ian. Could Jemma be the woman in the photograph on his credenza?

"Have you checked out the balcony?" Ian asked as they entered the great room.

"No. Not yet."

He took her arm and steered her through the crowd, greeting people as he passed.

When she stepped outside, the view roused her spirit. Once again the sun sprinkled golden accents on the water, and with Ian beside her, she was glad she had come. Though the sunset cheated them of one of the more dramatic shows, lilac and peach hues painted the bottom of the fluffy clouds.

A warm breeze ruffled the skirt of her dress, and she smoothed the fabric, then leaned against the railing and took in the full sweep of water, earth and sky. "It's beautiful. I'm sure it'll be difficult for Philip to move from here." She pivoted and eyed the sprawling upper windows that made up the penthouse. "But it's no place to bring up a child."

"I'm sure he's enjoyed it while he lived here. Time and experience change our lives—sort of what Philip said earlier." Ian leaned out and pointed down the beach. "You can see Philip's sailboat from here."

"Nice," she said, following the direction of his gesture. "Does Jemma sail?" The question left her before she stopped herself. Why bring up sailing or Jemma? Whether the photo in his office was Jemma or not, Esther didn't need to be compared to someone more flexible. More adventurous.

"She enjoys it, I think. Jemma came from a difficult family background. I suppose sailing and pleasures like that were alien to her before meeting Philip."

Esther paused. So Jemma's life had been different. The news surprised her. As Ian had said, time changed lives. Jemma's had changed for the good. Maybe Esther's life would take a turn one day.

"Look who's having fun."

Hearing her sister's voice, Esther pivoted toward the French doors. "Rachel." She brushed a stray hair from her cheek and motioned toward the water. "Lovely view."

"Nice," Rachel said.

Jeff stood at Rachel's side and slid his arm around her shoulder. "How would you like a place like this?" He nuzzled Rachel's hair with his cheek.

"I'd be happy anywhere with you," she said, tip-toeing to reach his lips with a quick kiss.

Embarrassed by their affection, Esther cleared her throat. "Rachel, have you met Ian Barry?"

"He's the one with the library card, if I remember correctly. We met at the restaurant downstairs." She extended her hand. "Nice to see you again."

Esther cringed at her forgetfulness.

"He's the assistant manager," Jeff said, his voice emphasizing the position. Still, he didn't hide his pleasure at finding Esther and Ian together. "Since you're in good hands, I think we'll go inside and let you two alone." He gave an obviously dumbfounded Rachel a wink, and they returned to the great room, arm in arm.

"See. It worked," Ian said. "They think I'm an enamored admirer." After he realized what he'd said, an uneasy look swept across his face. "Not that I'm not."

"You don't have to play the game with me, Ian." His attempt to cover his faux pas left Esther uncomfortable. She knew he had no real interest in her. He'd offered to be her friend and to save her from Rachel's matchmaking. That's all Esther expected. Yet a feeling of disappointment inched through her. What more did she want? Irritation replaced her dejection.

From his expression, Esther knew Ian felt uneasy, too. She wished she could say something to undo her remark, but nothing came to mind, and she focused on the sun sinking behind the horizon with the speed of a lead ball.

Darkness stretched across the water as quickly as spilled ink. People began to drift onto the balcony. Soon the fireworks lit the sky, made more magnificent by their reflection in the water. Rachel and Jeff stood beside her and Ian. Detecting a reminder in Ian's subtle look, Esther allowed him to slide his arm around her back and draw her closer while they praised the spectacular display.

His actions were all part of the game, she knew, but a secret feeling of pleasure settled in her stomach—a closeness and familiarity she'd never shared with anyone.

They think I'm an enamored admirer. Ian's words plowed through her thoughts. Grateful for the darkness, Esther struggled to hide her unsettled emotions.

Ian rested his back against the same chair he'd used on his last visit, but today, before he arrived, he'd reviewed his thoughts and feelings with care, then prayed he wouldn't do anything to distress Esther. He knew he'd upset her at the fireworks.

He'd enjoyed her company that day and relished the opportunity to be with her. For much of the evening they'd talked and laughed like two friends...until he'd made the ''enamored'' comment. Tonight he'd sensed her distance when he walked in the door. Why did a woman with such ability and control seem so sensitive at times?

Ian slipped off his glasses and pressed his fingers against his eyes. He'd hoped for so much that evening. A positive step toward a growing friendship. He remembered how the fireworks display had lit the sky, and how Esther's face had brightened as beautifully as one of the colorful explosions.

He'd enjoyed watching her excitement in the dusky balcony light—her look of pleasure watching the spectacle. Washed by the lamps from indoors, her shiny blond hair had been tousled by the breeze, and he'd longed to brush back the loose strands from her face. He'd thought of kissing her cheek as Rachel had done to Jeff. But Esther had stood rigid beside him, and he was in no position to admit his real feelings. He'd been rejected too many times to take the chance.

Ian looked at the dark glass frames in his hand. He hated the things, and he breathed a relieved sigh, knowing in another day or two he'd never wear them again.

He had an appointment for contacts, but he'd kept it as a surprise for Esther. One day, if he ever had the courage to kiss her, he didn't want his frames to interfere.

Esther's footsteps sounded on the landing, and she sailed into the room. "Here you go," she said, handing him a glass of iced tea.

She carried hers to the desk, set it on a coaster and flipped open the manila folder. "Now let's get down to business."

He struggled with what to say. He couldn't spend the evening paralyzed by the tension he sensed between them.

She sat across from him, her attention focused on papers she shuffled from one pile to the other. Finally she pulled out a couple of sheets. "Here they are."

She rose and rounded the desk. "These are the questions I listed for Mr. Somerville." She handed him the papers and headed back to her desk. "I need answers for them before I can proceed. He mentioned he'd gone over them with you."

Ian scanned the list, the answers lost somewhere beneath his concern. In the weighted hush he pulled together his thoughts. He longed to mend the feelings between them. But what could he say that wouldn't scare her off? He couldn't tell her how much he cared about her. She'd think it was another ploy or reject him without giving him a chance. *Lord, give me the words.*

Ian lowered the papers, his thoughts floundering. "Before we get into this, I'd like to talk about the other night, Esther."

"We fooled them, didn't we?" she said.

Her words rang in his ears like a death knell. If she'd wanted to get even, she had. "But there was more to it than that."

"More to it? No, Ian. I appreciate your efforts, and I hope it motivates them to lay off a while. I need a breather until I can figure out what to do with my father. I thought you did a good job letting them think I was someone special."

"But I do think you're special."

"It was a ploy…and it worked. Did you see their faces? Rachel and Jeff were all but dancing."

Grasping for a solution, Ian pulled together the strings of their conversation. Esther said she needed time to decide what to do, and he needed time to prove he really cared about her. "They'll stop dancing in a heartbeat when they don't see us together. Did you think of that?''

Her face drooped with awareness. ''Yes, but I'd hoped they'd lay off for a while. Somehow I have to—''

''Then why stop now? You said it worked. They looked thrilled seeing us together, and I do enjoy your company, Esther. That's not a joke.''

She stared at the floor. ''Thanks, but—''

''We're friends. Right?''

Lifting her eyes, she nodded. ''Yes. That's true.''

''Then let's act like friends.'' It sounded so easy to him. ''Look at it this way. We have to spend time together with this project. Why not make them aware of it? Like tonight...'' His pulse accelerated as the plan spilled into the air. ''You could mention I was here when you talk with Rachel. She doesn't have to know it's business.''

''But that's lying.''

''It's not lying. Let her make the assumption, not you.'' He felt exhilarated. ''Maybe one day when I'm off work...you could come to the marina. You said you might change your mind and try sailing again. That would look good. You know, a day out on the boat. That would seem like a date to Rachel.''

Esther's uncertain expression faded. ''Yes. That's true. I'm still not sure about the boat, but I see what you mean.''

His hope grew. ''It'll give you time. Time to decide what to do about your dad. I'm sure Jeff and Rachel will lay off the matchmaking if they believe you and I have struck up a...meaningful friendship.''

She took a deep breath, then sent it shuddering into the air.

Ian sat on the edge of his chair, waiting.

"Let me think about it," she said. "It feels like deceit to me, and I've never lied to my sister."

He rose and rested his palm against the desk, leaning forward to be near her. "But it's not a lie. I do enjoy your company. You enjoy mine. We need to be together on this project anyway. What do you say?"

Chapter Seven

Esther eyed her watch. Nearly time to leave. She pulled books from the bin, checked them in and made a neat pile. For the past few days since she'd talked with Ian, he'd lingered in her mind. They'd declared a friendship, and she had to admit she enjoyed his company...but along with the pleasure, she'd opened herself up, made herself vulnerable—one thing she thought she'd never do.

Rubbing her hand along the tension in her neck, Esther refocused on her work. She moved the stack of books to the library cart and turned back to the counter. Her stomach somersaulted when she saw him standing there.

"Ian."

"Hi," he said, a look of shyness on his face.

She paused and drew back. "Ian! Where are your glasses?"

He pointed to his eyes. "Contacts."

"You're kidding me."

"No. Thought I'd give these a try."

"You look great. I like you without glasses." She chuckled. "Not that I didn't like you before."

"You sound like me, trying to get your foot out of your mouth."

She chuckled at her blunder, admiring his new look, but admitting to herself he looked good with or without spectacles.

"I know you weren't expecting me," Ian said, "but I thought I'd take a chance and drop by."

"What's up?"

"I'm heading over to the marina, and I thought…you might like to come along with me."

Taking a quick look at her watch, she realized he'd timed it right. She'd be off in a few minutes.

"Before I left work I mentioned to Jeff I was stopping here to invite you. I'm adding grease to the wheels." He leaned back and rocked on his heels. "And as you see, here I am. No lies. It's a fact."

"But I haven't agreed to be part of this charade…let alone go sailing." Her heart joined her stomach in its flip-flop motion, and she wasn't sure if she felt hungry or nauseated.

"I know. It's okay, though. Don't you see? I asked you like I said I would. If Jeff tells Rachel and they make more of it than there is, it'll give you some ammunition. Right?"

What he said made sense, but uncertainty still wriggled through her. "I suppose."

He rested his elbows on the counter. "So? What do you think?"

Think? She couldn't even breathe. "I'm not sure, Ian. The sailboat? I—"

"We won't venture out too far from shore unless you're comfortable and…we'll have a picnic. While you change clothes, I'll pick up some food. We can be on the lake by seven. That gives us more than two good hours of daylight."

His enthusiasm made her grin. He was involved in this whole charade for her. How could she say no? "Okay, but if I panic, can we eat at the marina?"

He chuckled. "Sure." He stepped backward, aiming for the library doorway. "Okay. I'll pick you up at your place in about forty-five minutes. How's that?"

"Fine," she said, watching him pivot and dart through the doorway. When he'd vanished, fear jarred her. She hoped he didn't mind eating at the marina restaurant, because as reality settled in, that's what she feared might happen.

Ian helped Esther onto the boat, then carried the food on board. So far so good. The sky looked clear, and Esther's smile made the day perfect. When the food was stowed below in the galley, he retraced his steps up the ladder to the deck and started the engine.

"Would you help me cast off?" he said as he hopped back onto the pier.

Without a word, Esther followed his direction, and when he'd stepped back into the boat, he headed for the wheel, then maneuvered from the pier and down the channel toward the lake.

Occasionally he took the liberty of watching Esther. Though quiet, she leaned back with her face turned toward the sun. A gentle breeze ruffled her hair, and as she did so often, she reached up and tucked a few loose strands behind her ear.

Today she had on earrings, small golden hoops that wrapped around her earlobe. She'd dressed in a red knit top with a square neckline, and he watched her pull suntan lotion from her shoulder bag and rub it along her neck and arms to protect her fair skin. He'd noticed earlier her navy shorts had been decorated with little red anchors on the back pockets, and he sat back enjoying her sailor look as she squirted cream into her palm and worked the balm onto her legs.

He'd never seen her in shorts before, and his gaze was drawn to her trim, shapely legs as she plied them with lotion. Pulling his attention back to the lake, he chided himself for ogling and felt grateful she hadn't noticed.

"Would you like some?" she asked, extending the plastic bottle.

He glanced down at his browned arms, wondering if he really needed protection. "Want to take the wheel while I put some on?"

"I can do it for you," she said, rising from the bench and moving beside him. "Your neck is the most likely to burn, I think."

He held his breath, waiting in expectation until her cool hands rested on his skin, glided along his hairline, then down his neck. When she worked her way to the front, she gave his throat a playful squeeze.

"Strangle me, and you'll have to sail this boat

back to shore by yourself.'' He sent her a teasing grin.

''I think I could,'' she said, covering her palm with lotion and rubbing it along his arms.

He loved the feel of her gentle touch on his skin. The intimacy. Most of all, he loved having Esther at his side, bantering like a real friend.

''How are you doing out here on the lake?'' he asked, hoping he didn't create an unwanted reaction.

''I'm trying not to think about it,'' she said. ''You were right, though. It feels wonderful being on the water. It's been so long.''

When they'd reached the lake, he'd set his course closer to the shoreline than he normally would, knowing Esther would realize he was keeping his promise. ''Should I tie the wheel, or can you help me while I raise the sails?''

She motioned toward the bow. ''Steer into the wind, right?''

''Right. Think you can do it?''

She agreed and slipped into position at the wheel while he headed toward the winch to raise the sails. He moved from the mainsail to the staysail, then the jib. He tied off the last halyard and adjusted the sheets to trim the sails.

Returning to the cockpit, Ian stood a moment, admiring Esther at the wheel. She'd handled the vessel like a true sailor. He rested his hands on her shoulders ''Hungry?''

''Starving,'' she said. ''Want me to carry up the goodies?''

''If you can hang on a minute, I'll do it.''

She nodded, and he hurried down the ladder into the galley and brought up the picnic box. On deck he slid the container onto a bench. "I'll take over, and you dish it up. How's that?"

"Sounds good." At the moment she stood, a roller hit the hull, and the boat yawed, sending a new look onto her face—uncertainty heading toward distress.

"Getting nervous?" he asked.

She shrugged. "I'm pretending I'm fine." She sat on the bench, opened the lid and peeked inside.

He watched as she pulled out the plates, bucket of chicken, dinner rolls, raw vegetables, potato chips and a bag of cookies—not homemade, but touted to be as close as one could get. She loaded his plate, and he rested it on the settee beside him, eating with one hand while guiding the boat with the other.

When Ian realized she was staring at him, he faltered. "Something wrong?"

"No. I'm thinking about you...and your contacts."

Her comment puzzled him. "Is this going somewhere?"

She gave him an uneasy look. "I've been thinking. You're handsome to me with or without glasses. I can just see your eyes better without those thick lenses though."

Handsome? He'd never thought of himself as handsome. Words stuck in his throat until he dragged them out. "Thanks...but what brought that on?"

She shrugged. "Sometimes we let little things become so important. I remember your complaining about the glasses, and I realized—this is a lesson for myself, too—those little things on the outside don't mean anything. It's what's on the inside that counts.''

He nodded while her words settled in his thoughts, giving him a warm feeling. How many times had he looked at himself in the mirror and compared himself to more handsome men…like Jeff or Jim Mason? She'd given him food for thought. Food. He looked at his plate and, concealing his emotion, grabbed a carrot stick and gave it a firm crunch.

Esther grinned, but only nibbled on a dinner roll, and after time passed she slid onto the bench beside him. ''This is lovely, Ian, but do you think we could head back? I'm getting—''

''You've done fine. Really.'' He concentrated on tacking in a wide arc and aiming for the marina.

''Thanks,'' she said, looking more relieved as the boat came about and headed back. ''I'm sorry.''

''No need. It's been a great day.'' He meant every word. Though he'd expected her to decline again, she'd finally agreed to sail, and he was grateful for that.

''One day I hope to kick this panic, but I know it'll take time. Thanks for giving me the little push and inviting me to join you.''

''You're welcome. Any time.'' He took advantage of the flow of conversation to satisfy his curiosity. All day he'd wondered if she had decided to agree with his plan to discourage Rachel and Jeff's matchmaking. ''Then the day's served two purposes. You've been out on the lake, and it will give Rachel and Jeff something else to talk about.''

She smiled. "It will. I'm sure my phone will be ringing when I get home tonight."

Her comment pleased him. "Don't think you have to give them details. Just tell the truth. We spent an afternoon sailing. That alone should work. They'll get off your back, I'm sure."

"I hope so." Her expression turned thoughtful as she swung her legs to the bench. "Nothing like the sun, wind and water."

"And friendship," he added.

She didn't look his way, but he saw a smile curve her mouth. "And friendship."

"What do you think?" Jeff asked, filling a dish with ice cream from his freezer. "Are they spending time together only for the research…or could it be the real thing?"

Rachel grinned and ran her palms up his back. "It may have started as research, but that sailboat outing didn't involve any business I've heard about…except maybe monkey business."

Jeff turned to face her and grinned. "Well then, maybe we can stop our matchmaking and see what happens." Returning to the ice cream, he pressed on the lid and slid the carton into the freezer. When he turned back, he handed a bowl to Rachel and took one for himself.

She dipped in the spoon and let the cold dessert melt on her tongue. "It seems so strange to think of Esther with a man. She's been so standoffish I can't believe she did this on her own."

Rachel followed Jeff into the living room.

"You don't give your sister enough credit."

She plopped beside him on the sofa. "She's attractive enough. Beautiful, really. I wish I had her looks."

Jeff tousled Rachel's hair. "You? You're gorgeous."

"To you, maybe, but look at Esther. She's lovely. It's just her…well…her personality. She's all business and control. I'm surprised Ian got past all that to find the real woman underneath."

Licking his spoon, Jeff thought, then shifted to face her. "Ian hasn't been much of a Romeo, either. He rarely brought anyone to company activities. Not that I can remember." He started to chuckle.

"What's so funny?" She gave him an elbow poke.

"I don't suppose I ever told you. Ian's the dude who dated Jemma…or tried to…before she married Philip Somerville. Can you believe it?"

"Jemma? You're kidding." She poked him again, but harder this time. "That's not funny, Jeff. Think of how embarrassing it must be for him to work for Philip and know he was rejected by his wife."

Jeff shrugged and spooned out another mouthful of ice cream. "We all have our problems. You think I've never been rejected?"

"Don't tell me she rejected you, too."

"No, but you did. Remember?" A smug look rose on his face, and he chuckled at her.

"I did, didn't I? Oh well, I changed my mind."

"You did," he said, leaning forward and kissing her lips with his frosty mouth.

Delving back into her chocolate swirl, Rachel remembered the first time they met. He'd been so cute, but so cocky. She'd longed to date him, but gave him a firm no before she finally submitted to his charm.

"So let's get back to Esther," Jeff said. "I'm sure Jim Mason liked her. If you don't think this is anything serious with Ian, I'll suggest Jim give her a call."

"Why don't we wait a while? She sounded so happy when I talked with her on the phone. They had a picnic on the boat, and when she got nervous, he brought her back without a word. He's really nice and treats her great."

Jeff tilted his head and looked into the distance. "Maybe I'll give Jim a teaser call. You know, tell him to hang in there and I'll try to see what Esther thinks of him. That way I won't encourage him or discourage him."

"Can't you just let things be for now?"

"But I'm not waiting forever, Rachel. I've given you a ring and I want you to wear it. More than that, I want to get married...so we can have babies and a life together."

"Me, too, but please be patient. Just a little longer."

Jeff slid his arm around her shoulders. "I'll try to be. I'll really try, but I hope you hear me. I love you, Rachel, but I'm not going to wait forever. Either Esther falls in love, or you and I will elope."

His words slithered down her spine, and confusion turned her limbs to jelly. She couldn't elope, but she didn't want to lose him, either. She loved him and understood why his patience had faded. All she could do was pray Esther would fall in love. And soon.

"Thanks for coming along with me on this one," Esther said, sitting across from Ian in his office.

"You're welcome. It's the least I can do."

She struggled to keep her eyes from focusing on the photograph behind him on the credenza. He'd never told her the funny story about Jemma, and her curiosity rose every time she remembered his comment. But for some reason, she didn't have the nerve to ask. "How did you get Philip to let you come along?"

"I'm a good sweet-talker."

Though he joked, his words set Esther on edge. "I've heard some of your sweet-talking." Between getting her on the sailboat and agreeing to the matchmaker ploy, he'd definitely beguiled her.

Ian only grinned. "Interviewing Grand Haven Charters was a great idea."

"Thanks. I can learn so much more when I ask questions and get direct answers. And thanks for adding a few questions of your own. You thought of a couple things I hadn't considered."

"It gives us things to think about before we go up to White Lake and talk with the sailing adventure company," Ian said.

"Are you sure you want to take off the time?"

Ian rose and ambled across the room. He faced her, resting his palms on the chair arms. "It's not time off. It's time used in a different way. Don't worry.'' He chucked her under the chin. ''Philip already said I should go with you.''

His playful affection tingled down her spine, but she managed to keep herself focused. ''That's great. On sailing issues, you know so much more than I do.''

Her gaze drifted, and she glanced at the picture frame again, studying the photo and trying to remember what Jemma looked like. She'd seen her only briefly at the Fourth of July party, and the photograph had been taken years earlier. She couldn't be sure.

What she did know was that Ian and the woman had known each other well. She saw it in their faces. The kind of familiarity a person has only with someone special.

Courage rose in her. She was tired of being curious. She'd just ask him. ''Ian, I was wondering—''

''When we can go to White Lake?''

He'd anticipated the wrong question, and she waited.

Ian moved back behind his desk and eyed his calendar. ''Not next weekend. That's the Bay Breeze summer picnic. We can't miss that.''

She swallowed her original question, which tangled in his latest statement. ''What do you mean *we* can't miss that?''

''If you're my girl, then you'll have to go with me. Right?''

His comment addled her. ''But I'm not really your girl.''

''No one knows that.'' A wry grin settled on his

face. "Anyway, you'll have a blast. Food and games. All kinds of things."

"I don't like games," she said. Her double meaning hung in the air.

"But you like food."

He'd missed her innuendo, and she chuckled. "I can't deny that."

"Then it's settled." He rose from the desk and patted a file folder she'd given him. "I'll look over this Internet information and let you know what I think."

"That's fine," she said, sensing that he had to get back to work. She picked up her shoulder bag from the floor and rose. "Then I'll talk with you—"

"Wait a minute. I'm not letting you go yet." He rounded the desk and reached her side. "The boss'll want to know if the resort has enough property for the boat sheds...if that's what you recommend. I thought we'd take a walk along the beach, and we can talk about the layout."

Walk on the beach? She looked down at her shoes. He hadn't mentioned walking on the beach. "I'm not dressed for a beach hike." She swung her leg and pointed to her feet.

He eyed her dress shoes, then shrugged. "Ever walked barefoot on the beach?"

"Sure, but I have on...never mind." She tried to imagine her panty-hose-covered feet moving through the sand. She curbed the scowl growing on her face.

"I'm teasing. We can take the sidewalk...just to get an idea."

A warm flush rose up her neck. "Never thought

about a sidewalk.'' She hadn't been thinking about much of anything lately. Something as logical as a sidewalk had escaped her usually organized, well-tuned brain. Ian's effect on her turned her mind into a whirlpool.

She followed him down the hall, and when her heels hit the granite-tiled lobby, she noticed Jeff standing near the registration desk.

Apparently Ian had spotted him, too. As if they had held hands a lifetime, he slipped his fingers through hers as they crossed the wide expanse toward the outside door.

''What's up?'' Jeff called to them.

Ian halted. ''We're going out to look at the grounds. Esther's doing a research project for Philip.''

''I've heard,'' Jeff said. He gave Esther a wink. ''It's a nice day. Enjoy your walk.''

''I will,'' Esther said, her playful tone making its point. As soon as the words left her mouth, she cringed. How did God feel about her trifling with the truth? Though she and Ian were spending time together, their relationship had not been the romantic one that they were trying to convince her sister and Jeff it was.

With his hand entwined with Esther's, Ian led her through the doorway and down the slanted path to the lower sidewalk along the sand. Aware of Ian's palm against hers, Esther felt a pleasant tingle race up her arm, a sensation she oddly enjoyed. Yet knowing their act was only a scam, she knew the feeling should be ignored.

When they were away from the building, Esther let her hand drop from Ian's. "The coast is clear," she said, forcing a quick smile.

Ian glanced back toward the resort. "Maybe not. Jeff's curious. He might still be watching us, and he'll get suspicious if we don't look cozy."

Instead of grasping her hand again, he slipped his arm around her waist and moved closer to her side as they ambled along the sidewalk. The pleasant tingle she'd felt earlier generated into an electrical current that coursed along her frame. What was happening to her?

When they stopped midway along the sidewalk, Ian halted and pointed out the property line.

Esther struggled to think of boat sheds and docks, while her mind reeled with the heated current that charged through her.

This had to stop. She'd been without a man's company and attention forever. But now that she'd tasted the sweetness of a relationship, even the thought of being alone caused her to miss the companionship already.

"What do you think?" Ian asked.

Her muddied thoughts pulled snippets of information and earlier discussion from her seared brain, and she gave a response she hoped made sense.

"Once the recommendation is made," he said, "I can help you sketch up some rough schematics. Just so Philip gets the idea."

"That would be helpful. Thanks."

The wind blew her hair, and she tucked the wayward tresses behind her ear. While Ian's spicy citrus aftershave floated past her, tantalizing her, she realized her feelings had begun to change. Though the sun's warmth played on her skin, inside, icy tendrils of concern slithered through her.

The game Ian played had become *real* to Esther.

Chapter Eight

Ian spooned up a healthy portion of potato salad and ladled it next to his second bratwurst. He loved those German sausages and rarely ate them, so this was a treat.

Standing away from the picnic table unobserved, he regarded Esther. She'd worn jeans with a pink-and-blue-striped knit top, and as a joke, when he picked her up she'd worn a baseball cap—backward.

She'd told him how much she disliked sports, and he knew if she came to the picnic his co-workers would goad her into playing softball. In past years the game had been the highlight of the day. Avoiding the fact that she'd be miserable, Ian wanted Esther there anyway—for himself more than their charade.

Funny how Esther had gotten under his skin. He'd always admired her at the library. She seemed like a down-to-earth woman—someone who knew where to find the answer to anything, someone who had life under control. He'd seen that in her home. Even there, her organization and neatness gave her house a no-nonsense feeling. Just like Esther.

But Ian wished she could relax. Many times he'd wanted to tell her how he really felt about her. How his feelings had grown from admiration to something deeper. But he wanted no part of having Esther laugh in his face or tell him he'd misunderstood her intentions. He'd had that experience too many times before.

The day they'd walked along the beach he'd enjoyed holding her hand, but she'd dropped it as if she'd been asked to hold a toad. Somehow he'd tugged a little gumption from his resources and slipped his arm around her waist. The feeling nestled against his heart like a sleepy head against a downy pillow. He felt comfortable and complete with her at his side.

Pulling himself from his thoughts, Ian looked across the grass toward Esther. She was staring at him. He'd taken too long, dawdling with her in his thoughts. He gave her a wave and headed back.

"Hi," Ian said, lifting his leg over the plank seat and settling down beside Esther.

"Thought you got lost," she said, lifting the paper napkin to wipe her mouth. "Good food…just like you said."

He wanted to tell her the softball game would be fun, too. Instead, he only nodded and took a bite of the *brat*.

"Those things are delicious," she said. "But I'm too full to have another. I saved room for some watermelon."

"What? No pie?" He gave an admiring glance at her slender frame.

"Fruit's better for the figure." She patted her belly, as if she were overweight.

Her figure looked great to him, but he kept his mouth shut.

She rose, and he watched her walk to the buffet table, returning soon with a slice of melon. With her fork she flicked out the seeds, then cut off a chunk and slipped it into her mouth.

Ian gazed at her, noticing her lips were as naturally rosy as the watermelon. She ran her tongue over them to catch the juice, and his muscles tensed, thinking of her in his arms.

"Sweet as sugar," she said, flicking out a few more seeds and lopping off another piece.

To Ian, she was sweet as sugar.

"The seedless sound like a good idea, but have you eaten one?" she asked.

His mind had halted at her soft lips, and when her words soaked in, it took a moment to grasp what she'd said. "Never had one."

"They're not sweet like this. Try a piece." She selected a bright red section and sliced her fork into the juicy pulp, then lifted the sizable chunk to his mouth.

Watching her eyes focus on his mouth and her hand guiding the fork to his lips sent his heart on a romp. If he dismissed his good sense for one moment, he'd take her in his arms and experience the feeling of her sugary lips against his.

But Ian tried to be a practical man. Instead, he

opened his mouth and accepted her offering. She'd been correct. The melon tasted as she'd described.

She grinned and pulled the fork away, returning her attention to flicking away the seeds.

When the food had dwindled and the leftovers were stored, people were roused to get the game started. Ian rose, stretched his arms over his head and did a couple of knee bends and toe touches for exercise.

"Ready, partner?" he asked, yanking her baseball cap from the table and plopping it on her head.

"Not me," she said, holding her hands up to push him away. "I'm a spectator." She pulled off the cap and dropped it on the table. "This was a joke."

"Sorry. You can't be." He stood beside her, tapping his foot.

"What do you mean?"

"They won't let you. Everyone plays...except a couple of elderly ladies. You're not elderly."

"I'm much older than I look," she said, clinging to the table.

Rachel and Jeff headed their way, and Rachel's voice sailed to meet them. "Come on, Esther. It's all in fun."

Esther sent her sister a glowering stare. "Let's define fun."

"Be a good sport. Come on," Jeff said, beckoning her to follow.

A few others began to taunt her as Ian had feared, and with purposeful slow motion, Esther slid her legs over the plank seat and stood. She plopped the cap on her head and spun it around sideways. "You'll live to regret this," she said to Ian.

Her faint smile eased his worry while she dragged along beside him.

They split into teams—the Bays and the Breezes—then decided positions. Since the Bays won the toss and were at bat, Ian flung Esther a glove. "You're second base and I'm at first."

She glowered at him.

He pointed to the second-base bag. "Smile. You're having fun."

She marched to second base, and in a few minutes the game began.

Struggling to keep focused on the play, Ian preferred to watch Esther. She'd donned her mitt and stood with one foot on the bag, her hands resting on her thighs. For a woman who hated sports, she looked as if she knew what she was doing.

When the Bays hit a line drive, the shortstop reached for the ball, but missed. To Ian's amazement, Esther leaped into the air and caught the ball.

"Out," came the call.

The next plays went fast, and with no score, the Breezes were up to bat.

Ian headed for Esther and clamped his hand on her shoulder. "I thought you hated sports."

"I do."

"But you look like you know what you're doing. I couldn't believe when you caught that ball."

"I didn't say I've never played," she said, smacking her fist into the mitt. "I just hate it. I don't like competition."

He squeezed her shoulder. "You're amazing." To Ian, Esther seemed like a locked box with all kinds of wonderful things inside, but no one had the key. Today he'd had a brief peek, reveling in her wealth of surprises. Pride settled in his chest. His girl and his team.

His girl. She wasn't his girl…yet. He'd had a long talk with God about Esther. But all that seemed clear was to give her time.

The game flew, and each inning made Ian gape with pleasure at the woman who'd told him she didn't like competition.

The opposing Bays had moved ahead in the sixth inning. When the Breezes came up to bat, Ian bristled with determination. He pulled out his handkerchief and mopped his forehead. Pressure was on. The first two batters had failed to get on base.

When Ian headed for the plate, Jeff strolled to his side and plopped his hand on Ian's shoulder. "Let's get serious. Try to hit the ball between the second and third baseman. They're both bungling."

Ian chuckled. His aim was to hit the ball. The direction would be a surprise. "Sure thing, Jeff."

Jeff stepped away, and Ian took a couple of practice swings, then stepped up to bat.

He eyed the pitcher, and as the ball shot toward him, he swung.

"Strike one," the umpire called behind him.

He concentrated on the pitcher. This time the ball came in low, and Ian shifted his leg to miss it.

"Ball one."

He riveted his focus on the pitching mound, ready. This time it was high.

"Ball two."

Ian calculated. He'd thrown him two balls, slow and easy. Speculating, he looked for a fast, straight ball. Ian tightened his stance, waiting.

The ball barreled toward him. Like a wound spring, Ian let the bat fly. The whack resounded, and the ball soared. Ian didn't hesitate. He dropped the bat and ran for first. The first baseman stood alert, waiting for the ball. Ian flew past first and slid into second just before the second baseman's catch.

His team cheered, and he braced his left hand on his thigh and wiped away the perspiration from his forehead with the other.

Esther came up to bat. She'd shifted her cap, and now the bill was in back.

Ian grinned, but no smile softened Esther's look. Grasping the bat high over her right shoulder, she waited at the plate, her trim legs extended in a confident stance, her eyes on the ball, the bat ready to spring.

On second base, Ian squinted at the pitcher, then looked at Esther and held his breath.

The pitcher's arm shot forward as the ball tore from his hand, low, straight and fast.

But Esther had anticipated the pitch. Lowering her stance, she hit the ball with a crack, and her legs propelled her forward before Ian had gotten his bearings. With the ball heading for right field, Ian pushed off the bag and raced to third, then home.

When the dust settled, Esther stood on second base, and the Breezes had evened the score.

Jim Mason came to the plate and smashed the ball beyond the left fielder. Esther passed third, then crossed home plate, and Jim followed, moving their score up two runs.

Amid the cheers, Ian pulled Esther into his arms, giving her a giant hug. "You're a trouper."

"That's why I hate competition. I'm not a happy loser," she said.

Her response gave him a good laugh, and he tousled her hair as she stepped aside.

"Give the lady a kiss for that run," a voice called out.

He chuckled and caught Esther's hand, knowing Jeff's and Rachel's attention was glued to their actions.

"If you don't, I will," Jim said, giving Ian a nudge.

Esther blanched. Her gaze clung to his as if she was wondering what he would do. Trying to look as if he'd done it a million times, Ian drew her into his arms and lowered his lips to hers, to cheers of encouragement. He drew back in a heartbeat, but the warmth of her mouth and the softness of her lips lingered.

Smiling at the crowd, Esther stepped away. But Ian noticed the flush on her neck and the unsteady movement of her step. He'd flustered her. But was the reaction positive or negative? Had she enjoyed the kiss...or resented it? With no time to ponder his question, he stepped out of the way for the next batter.

By the bottom of the ninth inning, the game was tied—eight all. "Okay, this is it," Ian said, moving into step with Esther. "One more run and the game's over."

"I'll do that myself just to get this finished."

"Oh, come on," he said, sliding his arm around her waist, "you're enjoying every minute of this."

She lifted an eyebrow. "I am? Funny. I didn't know that."

He'd enjoyed every minute of it. Being with her...and the kiss. The memory washed over him. He prayed the experience wouldn't put a new barrier between them as so many things had. "I hope you understood about the kiss. I didn't have much..."

She glanced at him, then looked away. "You didn't have any choice. I understand."

Did he hear disdain in her voice? He'd have kissed her on his own if she'd invited it. Everything he did left him uncertain.

When Ian came up to bat, a man was on second. If he could get a good hit, their team could score the winning run.

He eyed the pitcher, trying to read his behavior. Thinking back to his pattern, he expected a low pitch, then a high, before coming home for a strike. Ian took his place and readied his stance.

The ball shot forward.

"Strike one."

Strike? He narrowed his eyes, taking in the pitcher. The guy had fooled him. He'd be ready next time.

The ball sailed toward him. With assurance he swung and missed.

"Strike two."

His confidence sinking into the ground, Ian faced the pitcher. He took a calming breath, then lifted the bat.

The ball came at him straight and slow. Ian timed his swing, and as the ball dropped into place, he thrust the bat forward, heard the thwack and headed for first.

"Out."

He skidded to a halt and looked at the pitcher holding his pop-up.

With his head hanging, Ian strode back to the team and studied Esther as she marched forward. She'd said she hated to lose, and even though this was only a sandlot game, he hated defeat, too.

Esther had turned her cap around, the bill low on her forehead. With the bat dangling at her side, she stood a moment facing the mound, like a judge weighing the sentence.

With calculated motion she lifted the bat, her fingers wrapping around the wood. She adjusted her stance and waited.

Not to be buffaloed, the pitcher followed her precision moves. He adjusted his cap, settled his feet in the dirt and paused, the ball resting in his mitt. In a flash of motion he pulled back, and with the snap of his wrist the ball headed for Esther. Her body responded to the action, and her bat plowed forward, smacking the ball in a line drive to center field.

Esther flung the bat aside, raced around the bases

and crossed home plate behind the runner from second base, who had scored the winning run.

Ian dashed forward, catching Esther in his arms, but this time as if prepared, she paused, tilting her head upward, and captured his gaze. With her look so direct, he froze, unable to lower his mouth to hers.

"Great game," he muttered.

"You, too. Thanks." She slid from his arms.

Irritated with his ineptness, Ian grabbed his mitt from the ground and tossed it into the equipment box. He followed behind, joining the team with hugs and laughter, celebrating their win.

But Ian's focus was on Esther. Her gaze drifted to him, then turned away. Had he seen disappointment in her face?

"We're pretty good," Jeff said, his arm around Rachel.

"Esther, you were royal," Rachel said.

Ian slipped his arm around Esther's shoulders and drew her to his side. "She was, wasn't she?"

"I just hate to lose," Esther said.

With Jeff and Rachel observing their every move, Ian took advantage. He grasped his courage and lowered his mouth to Esther's, this time in a kiss that lingered.

When he eased back, Esther's eyes remained closed, and he sensed she'd enjoyed every second of it. Her lids fluttered, then opened, and his heart soared with the look he saw in her eyes.

"We have to talk," she whispered.

He nodded, excited that he'd finally be able to tell her the truth.

Chapter Nine

Esther stared into the dusk through her window, confused and unsettled. She'd tried to talk with Ian after the picnic, but she'd blundered and ended up saying the opposite of what she meant—so she'd given up.

Either she had to learn to enjoy their friendship without any expectations or end it. Living alone so long, she'd become stubborn and controlling. When something didn't fall into her pattern, her approved system, she pushed it away.

Years ago she'd realized she pushed people away before they had a chance to do the same to her...so she could feel in charge. But for once in her life, she didn't want to push away anyone, and that anyone was Ian. He made her laugh and gave her life a different purpose besides helping library patrons find the references they needed.

Locating books and information once had given her a feeling of contentment and her life meaning.

Not anymore. She went to work each day hoping Ian might drop by, then went home hoping he'd call.

She still hadn't shed her fear of sailing. Ian would never give up his love of the sea...and she really didn't expect him to. The day they'd spent on Lake Michigan had brought back nostalgic loving memories of her family. Her uncle particularly. He'd been fun and full of life. When he'd died, part of her had died, too.

That was the day she'd questioned God. Why did so many evil people live when good, kind people died in needless boating accidents? Her logic had furnished an answer. Humankind did not think like God. If they did, they'd be God. She'd read so often in the Bible that everything had a purpose. But her heart had wanted to understand the purpose. Her heart had wanted an answer.

Just as her heart did today. She needed answers. Besides being concerned about Ian, she knew her sister dwelled in her mind. Rachel had phoned and asked to drop by. Esther could guess why—she'd seen the look in Jeff's face more and more. The man wanted his bride. He wanted a wife and family. Esther couldn't blame him.

The telephone rang, and she headed for it, wondering if Rachel had changed her mind. She said hello, and held her breath when she heard Ian's voice.

"You said we should talk...and I think we should," he said. "Can I come over?"

Her pulse thumped in her temple, and she looked

at the clock. "Rachel's dropping by any minute. This isn't a good time."

"Later, then?"

His request pressed her to the wall. "I don't know how long she'll be here, Ian." Esther also couldn't decide what to talk about anymore. What did she want from Ian?

The line was heavy with silence.

"I can phone you if she leaves early," Esther added.

He expelled a lengthy breath over the wire. "Okay."

"I'll call as soon as she leaves."

"Thanks," he said, and hung up.

What would she say to him? Should she end the charade before he did? Should she ask him to continue playing the game despite her heightened emotions? If she could just get her father to think rationally. That's what she longed for. His philosophy made no sense at all.

A noise sounded at the door, and Esther hurried to the kitchen as Rachel stepped inside. "Hi," she said, her eyes shifting away from Esther's gaze.

"Let's sit in the living room," Esther said, motioning toward the archway. "How about some iced tea?"

"Sure. Thanks."

Rachel went ahead of her into the living room, and Esther filled two glasses, anticipating their conversation, which she knew would be emotional…and stressful.

When she stepped into the room, Rachel glanced up, then looked away and evaded Esther's eyes.

After handing her the tea, Esther settled into a chair. "You look upset."

Her sister shrugged. "Jeff and I had another argument."

Knowing what was coming, Esther took a long drink of tea, giving her time to calm herself. "Over the engagement?"

"What else?"

"I don't know what to say, Rachel. I've done as much as I can." She'd done more than she ever thought she would, and now she'd agitated her own life trying to meet her sister's needs. "What's Jeff want you to do?"

"Elope." Finally she looked at Esther. "You know I can't do that."

"I know."

"He said if things don't change soon he's giving up."

"Giving up?" The thought sent a wave of nausea through Esther. "He wouldn't do that."

"I never thought he would, but..." Tears pooled in Rachel's eyes and rolled down her cheeks. "I don't know anymore."

"I can't work miracles. You know that." Esther clasped the bridge of her nose, praying for the right words. "I don't know what the future holds for me, Rachel. I'm spending time with Ian." She thanked the Lord for giving her the encouraging, yet careful words. "He's a nice man."

Silence hung on the air as Rachel lifted her head slowly. "Do you love him, Esther?"

Her plaintive voice sent a lump to Esther's throat. How could she answer that question? Was it love she felt, or was it only infatuation? Or could it be delirium over someone who finally thought her interesting enough to ask for her company? Esther sent up a plea to God for help.

"Esther?"

"It's too soon to know that, Rachel. We've only been seeing each other for little more than a month. How do I know?"

"But how do you feel about him? Do you want to be with him when he's not around? Do you think about him when he's not with you?"

Rachel's questions startled Esther. Was her sister defining love? Swallowing her confusion, Esther answered, "Yes, I feel lonely sometimes…and I miss his company."

With her admission, Rachel's face brightened. "It sounds like love. Don't you think?"

"Love takes two people with the same desire. I'm only one. I can't speak for Ian." Esther wished her sister would drop the subject and talk about what they could do to make things better. Brainstorm how to handle their father. Anything.

"I think Ian's crazy about you," Rachel said, hope filling her face. "How can you question his feelings? He's so sweet and he looks content when you're together." Again her eyes begged Esther to agree.

"That might be, but I can't make any predictions. Please don't put me on the spot."

Rachel's face wrestled with emotion. "Have you told Dad about Ian? How nice he is and that you're dating? Maybe if Dad thought there was hope he'd have a change of heart."

They both knew better than that. Esther's stomach churned with her sister's queries. "No, I've never mentioned him. I told Dad I was doing a big research job for Bay Breeze. You know Dad. He was interested in that and asked a million questions."

Rachel shifted forward, leaning closer as if lessening the distance between them would result in the answer she wanted. "Would you?"

"Would I what?"

"You know. Would you tell Dad about him? Better yet, take Ian to meet Dad. Just casually. Tell him you were in the neighborhood and decided to drop by. I think if he saw the two of you together…that might make a difference."

"Oh, Rachel." Esther bit her tongue, wanting to tell her it would make no difference at all. She wanted to shake her. But looking into Rachel's sad eyes, Esther lost her courage. "Don't ask me to do something like that. Please. That would be lying. Lying is sinful. We don't do that in this family."

"It's not lying. It's introducing your father to the man you're dating. Why is that lying?"

Esther fell back against the sofa cushion. "You're putting me on the spot, and I don't like it."

Rachel leaped from the chair and knelt at Esther's feet. "You know I'd do anything for you if you needed me." Her eyes filled with tears again.

"Stop it, Rachel. I'll see what I can do. Let me

figure out something.'' The pain churning in her stomach rose and settled in her heart.

''Thank you. I'm desperate, Esther. Jeff's desperate.'' Rachel rested her forehead on the armrest and picked at the nubs on the upholstery.

Esther shook her head. No one could be as desperate as she felt at that moment.

Ian pulled into Esther's driveway, turned off the lights and engine, then rested his head on the steering wheel. He'd been relieved when Esther phoned to tell him Rachel had left, but now he feared the conversation he and Esther were about to have.

She wanted to talk. He wanted to talk. But did they want to talk about the same thing? Esther had stumbled over some dialogue after the picnic, but she'd contradicted herself. Finally she'd given up and withdrawn again. Being with Esther seemed like a rollercoaster ride. Things went smoothly and slowly, but all the while, Ian knew they would reach a peak and things would go downhill.

He remembered the day she'd called him handsome. *I've been thinking. You're handsome to me with or without glasses.* He'd felt wonderful, realizing that she was right. What's inside is more important. Then in the next breath she said something that confused him.

Maybe the relationship wasn't worth it. Admiring Esther from afar seemed easier. Back then, he'd often sit in the library and wonder what it would be like to spend time with her, talking about all kinds of things. She seemed to know so much. Other times, he looked at her delicate frame and longed to slip his arm around her waist…or taste the sweetness of her tempting lips.

But dreams and reality weren't the same. They did have fun talking about things, but whenever she relaxed and began to accept their friendship something happened and her tension would rise again. Tonight he felt sure she would say goodbye. Their relationship would be strictly business.

He lifted his head and slapped the steering wheel. Sitting here like a coward served no purpose. He pushed open the car door and stepped into the night air. The scent of summer heat and warmed soil hovered over him. He slammed the car door, then went to the house and tapped on the screen.

From inside, the silence changed to footsteps, and soon Esther stood on the landing, unlatching the door. "Hi," she said, pushing it open.

Though she grinned at him, she looked stressed, and he remembered Rachel's visit. "Is everything okay?"

"Sure. Everything's fine." She locked the screen and followed him into the kitchen.

How could he respond? Obviously she wasn't telling him the truth. Something was wrong.

She headed for the refrigerator, then stopped and turned to face him. "Things aren't fine at all. I just had a horrible hour with Rachel."

Encouraged by her honesty, he neared her and rested his hand on her shoulder. "I'm sorry. It must have been serious."

"The engagement. Jeff's tired of waiting. It's the

same story.'' She turned back, opened the refrigerator and pulled out a pitcher of iced tea. ''Would you like some?''

''Sure,'' he said, scrutinizing the tension in her posture. He ached for her.

''I don't know what I can do to help.''

Ian knew what she could do. Fall in love and marry. He looked at her with longing, wishing he had captured her heart. Wishing things could be different.

She poured the liquid into a glass and handed it to him. ''Let's sit in the living room.''

He strode through the doorway, and, seeing her filled glass on an end table, he chose a nearby chair and sat.

Esther sank into the seat cushion and shook her head. ''I'm not in a very good mood. Sorry.''

''No problem. Tonight probably isn't a good time for us to talk.'' He leaned back, his mind swirling with possibilities. ''I have a hard time understanding all of this. I wish I knew your dad. I'd like to meet him.''

Esther's heart skipped a beat, then bounded to a gallop. She couldn't believe what he'd said…almost as if God were directing their conversation. ''What good would that do?''

''I don't know. I'd have a better idea what you're up against.'' He chuckled. ''I'm making your dad sound like the enemy.''

''He's a good father, but sometimes he does seem like an adversary. He's a character. Stubborn as a mule.''

A few seconds passed while she gathered her

thoughts. She'd spent hours trying to decide if she should push Ian away before he told her he wanted out of her problems. Now she sensed God moving her in another direction. A direction that could complicate her life even more. "If you'd like to meet him, come with me on Sunday. I'm going to church with him, then cooking his dinner."

"Sunday? Church and dinner? Don't you think he'd find it odd to bring me along?"

"He'd love the company. Dad enjoys conversation."

His face was thoughtful for a moment. "Sure. Why not?"

She released a pent-up breath.

Folding his hands across his stomach, Ian stretched out his legs, resting his shoes on their heels, and sent her a tender smile.

He looked comfortable and content. Without hesitation, he'd agreed to meet her dad…so why did apprehension poke at her?

"Feel better?" he asked.

"Not better, but at least you'll understand what I'm going through. That helps."

"Misery likes company," he said.

"I suppose you can put it that way." She grinned, and it felt wonderful. She took a sip of tea, wondering if she should bring up their original purpose for getting together.

After a lengthy silence, Ian tucked in his legs and rested his elbows on his knees. "You wanted to talk."

Not anymore, she didn't. Or did she? So many

things needed to be out in the open. "I suppose I did." She rubbed the bridge of her nose, trying to find the words. "I guess I feel tense sometimes because...well...I worry that you're spending all this time with me and you'd much rather be doing something else."

"What else do you think I'd rather be doing?"

He had bypassed an answer with a question, and the reason concerned her. "Sailing...or spending your time with someone else."

"I'm sailing this weekend. You're welcome to come along. In fact, Jeff's hinted that he and Rachel would like an invitation."

"Jeff and Rachel?" That put her on the spot. "What did you say to Jeff?"

"I told him I'd see if you're free and would like to come along." A gentle look settled on his face. "I didn't know if you were ready to try again."

Was she ready? A shudder ran through her. "I don't know. I enjoyed the day we sailed, but I ruined it for you by getting jumpy."

"Maybe having Jeff and Rachel with us would distract you. Help you focus on something other than the old memories."

She shrugged. "Maybe. I don't know."

"If you'd prefer, I can tell him no."

Guilt knotted in her chest. Rachel and Jeff's problems might be soothed if they had something else to think about...like a day on the boat. "Don't tell Jeff no. It might be fun for them, and I know they could use the distraction."

"Then you'll go?"

She bit the inside of her lip, trying to pull the answer from her throat. Finally she nodded.

"That's great, Esther. I'll let Jeff know tomorrow. It should be fun." He shifted in the chair. "So let's get back to this talk. Who do you think I want to be with?"

"I don't know. I'm the one who's settled on being single...not you. Maybe you should find someone that—"

"Maybe that's something I should worry about and not you. If I didn't enjoy your company, I wouldn't be here."

But that didn't answer her question. How did he feel about her? Did he have someone else in his life—someone he'd want as a marriage partner? The questions struck her like a stick. What difference did it make? She'd set her mind to be single. What difference was there if Ian had another woman in his life...or women, for that matter?

The credenza photograph rose in her mind. Could that picture be related to the Jemma story she'd never heard?

"What is it?" Ian asked. "You're thinking about something."

Courage shot through her. "It's your credenza."

"My what?"

"The photograph...the one with you and a woman. I wondered if that was Jemma."

He frowned a moment, then his face brightened, and he chuckled. "Why would you think that's Jemma?"

She shrugged, hoping to cover the discomfort that

rifled through her. "I don't know. You mentioned a funny story about her."

"Right. I forgot. I was going to tell you about that." Ian shifted in the chair and leaned closer. "Would you like to know about that woman? The one in the photograph?"

Esther's heart rose to her throat.

She nodded.

Chapter Ten

"It's my sister," Ian said, viewing Esther's confusion. "She lives in Colorado. Ever been there? It's great country."

"Your sister? I didn't know you had a sister."

"Lots of things you don't know." He realized his joke hadn't worked.

Esther's expression shifted to concern. "You're right. I know nothing about you. Nothing at all."

"I've told you about my dad." He sent her a hopeful look. "I've never had reason to talk about my sister. The picture you saw in my office was taken one fall afternoon near Vail while I was visiting her. Her husband took it."

"She's married."

"Yes, not everyone is single in my family. Only me. She has two kids. A boy and a girl. I'm crazy about them." Mentioning the kids sent his heart to the Colorado mountains. Though love traveled miles, he missed them.

"I've never been to Colorado."

Her comment seemed disjointed and uncomfortable.

"You should go sometime," he said. "Mountains, streams, deer and elk running wild."

"It sounds nice." She lowered her head for a moment. "I'm sorry about my question. I didn't mean to sound suspicious…and it's not my business anyway. You'd mentioned Jemma, and I saw the photograph…although after meeting her at the party, I should have realized she wasn't the woman in the picture." A disconcerted look moved across her face.

His stomach tightened as the pieces fell together. If she were curious about his relationship with another woman, then maybe she did care about him after all—even more than he had the courage to dream. He could never tell from her hot-and-cold behavior, but her question left him hopeful.

"Since you mentioned it, I'll tell you the funny story about Jemma."

Interest rose on her face. "Sure. I've wondered."

"Strange, but I didn't realize what was happening until it was over. Then I wanted to kick myself."

She nestled her legs beneath her, looking cozy and ready, as if waiting for a long tale.

"Jemma was the daughter-in-law of Philip's cousin, Claire, who owns a shop on Washington. You may have shopped there. Loving Treasures."

"Only once or twice."

"Anyway…Philip's a generous man and apparently helped set up Claire in the boutique business. He must have taken Jemma under his wing, too, thinking she was too young to be a widow. So he decided to play matchmaker...." He chuckled. Apparently that was a common goal, now that he thought about it.

"Sounds familiar," Esther said, a smile curving her mouth. "But don't tell me..."

"Yes. It's true—Philip seemed to think I'd make a perfect husband for Jemma. He had us spending time together on all kinds of projects."

"Did you like her?"

"I did, but no matter how I tried, we just didn't click. Anyway, after I opened my eyes, I could see right through the situation. She was crazy about Philip and he was nuts about her." The embarrassing memories hovered in his mind.

"So what was the problem? Why didn't he go after her himself?"

"Philip is nearly twenty years older than Jemma. And I don't think he considered himself good husband material...especially for a young woman."

"But it was meant to be. They're happy together...and now they're having a baby."

Esther had nailed the truth. Jemma and Philip were happy. Ian wondered what his life might have been like if things had worked out for him and Jemma. Would he be anticipating fatherhood today like Philip? An unexpected desire tugged at his chest. The image of his sister's children hung in his thoughts, then his solitary life swallowed him. He didn't like the picture.

Esther uncurled her legs, and a scowl covered her face. "How did you react to all that? Did you feel uncomfortable around her after being rejec—when she and Philip got together?''

She'd bitten off the word, but rejection rang loud and clear in Ian's head. He had been rejected again. ''No one likes to feel they've been a failure. I suppose I felt a little uncomfortable at first.''

''But you weren't a failure.''

''I wouldn't call it a success.''

''No, but it just wasn't God's design. The Lord has other plans for you.'' Her scowl had vanished, replaced by a look of tenderness.

''Any idea what they are?''

Her eyes widened, and she straightened her back. ''How would I know? I'm not even sure where my life is headed.''

''I thought God wanted you to be single. Isn't that what you told me?''

She lowered her gaze and remained silent for a moment as if she were unsure. ''Yes…that's what I've thought. I could have been wrong, but it's too late now.''

''Why is it too late now?''

''My life is settled. I have my own ways. It seems too difficult to change it all now.''

''You're not fifty, Esther. Philip was nearly fifty when he married Jemma. She was just about your age.''

An uneasy look loomed in her eyes.

''And I think Philip and Jemma are a perfect couple,'' Ian said.

''You do?''

''Yes. In fact, I think it was God's doing.'' Ian

relaxed against the cushion and grasped the iced tea. The brisk taste cleared his thoughts. "You know, Esther, sometimes I think you and I miss the obvious, trying to make human sense out of the Lord's business. We want to do God's bidding...but instead, we look so hard we miss it altogether. God's will goes right over our heads."

A thoughtful look rose in her eyes. "That could be."

"You should rethink things," Ian said. "Maybe God has a different direction for you than you thought." His heart thundered in his chest. He wanted so badly to tell her that he wanted to forget the charade and make their relationship the real thing...but he needed to be assured.

A rosy tint blossomed on her cheeks. "The Bible says God has a purpose for each of us. I think we've hit on something important today, Ian."

"We have?" His chest tightened as he contemplated what she would say. Had she decided her purpose was to be with him?

"Would you like to know what I figured out?"

"Sure." He studied her face, eager to hear what he hoped she was about to say. "What is it?"

"You said you'd like to meet my father?"

Her words fell on him like dust. He found nothing solid in her comment. "What do you mean?"

"Rachel thought if my dad saw us together, he might think that...something could come from our friendship. Something more serious and..."

"And he might be more understanding with Rachel. Is that it?" Ian's heart sank. He had hoped that for once her thought was about them. Something about their relationship being guided by God. Not more concern about Jeff and Rachel.

"Don't you see? I figured it was impossible to ask you to visit my dad, and you volunteered. Can't you see? Each deed we do has a purpose. I think that was God's doing."

Disappointment flooded over him. Oh, Esther. I think God's doing so much more…and you're missing the obvious, he thought.

The sailboat moved along the channel, and Ian watched the three others enjoying the perfect late-summer day. While Rachel and Esther leaned back with their legs stretched out along the bench, Jeff sat perched on the cabin top, scouting the shore through binoculars.

Ian had decided to make the best of things. If Esther had no interest in him, maybe God's purpose had been to help her get over her fear of sailing. Or maybe it was to make things right for Jeff and Rachel. As Esther had said a couple nights ago, the Bible said for everything there was a purpose. Maybe he'd been misguided, thinking he and Esther might have a future together.

Ian looked into the sky. Though the sun glistened off the water and its rays warmed their skin, a dark cloud hovered off in the distance. He'd have to keep an eye on it. He realized if Esther noticed she'd want to turn back.

Without frightening Esther, he'd mentioned a few safety rules to all of them in passing. He really had

no concerns about Esther or Rachel. They'd both
sailed when they were kids. But Jeff had never been
on a cutter. His cocky, playful manner alerted Ian to
keep a watchful eye on him.

Ian's attention drifted his way. Jeff lowered the
binoculars and winked at Rachel. "Sitting here, I'm
missing out on you...and some sunshine romanc-
ing."

Jeff discarded the binoculars on a bench and eased
his way over to Rachel. Sliding his arm around her
shoulder, he gave her a quick kiss, then tilted her
head against his. Nestled together, they murmured to
each other with an occasional chuckle or a teasing
poke.

Esther sat alone, looking into the horizon. A hint
of concern tugged at her mouth, but she covered it
well, and Ian pushed away any thought of asking her
if they should head to the marina. If she wanted to
go back, she'd say so.

"Hey, Esther. Why are you sitting there alone?"
Jeff asked. "How about cuddling up with the captain?"

She pulled herself up straight. "Remember the
rules of the road. No matter what vehicle, drivers
keep their hands on the steering wheel," she said, a
faint grin brightening her face.

Ian caught her subtle look and beckoned to her. If
they were trying to convince Jeff and Rachel they
were falling in love, they'd have to look the part.

Esther accepted his offer. She rose and nestled
beside him, resting her back against the cockpit
coaming.

Ian noticed Rachel's watchful gaze and slid his arm around Esther's shoulders. "They're watching us."

Esther leaned toward him. "Do you know what I just realized?" she murmured. "Jeff's a little immature, don't you think?"

He grinned. "They're younger. I guess it's expected."

Without alerting her, Ian studied the sky, realizing the dark cloud had grown high overhead. Wisdom told him to start back before a storm whipped up, and he prayed they would reach the marina before it became serious. Already the swells had risen, and he feared the wind against the tide, not a good situation for his small cutter.

Hoping to distract Esther while he came about, he scrambled for conversation. He'd noticed her thoughtful look and asked, "Something on your mind?"

"Are you still coming on Sunday?"

He wondered what had motivated the question. "Why not? You promised me a home-cooked meal."

"Aren't you lucky," she said. "Or should I say aren't I lucky?"

Her playful response heartened him. He nuzzled his lips against her ear while his pulse thundered. "I know I am."

Esther shrank from him with a giggle. "That tickles." Her voice carried on the breeze.

"Hey," Jeff said, "that's what this lady needs. A little tickling." He snuggled Rachel's neck until she twisted and wiggled to make him stop.

Jeff didn't give up, and Rachel slipped off the bench, laughing.

"Careful," Esther called, "one of you'll get hurt."

Ian sensed Esther's concern. "Better slow down the roughhousing. Your sister is getting nervous."

Rachel grinned at her from the deck.

"Aye, aye, Captain," Jeff said, leaping up and offering his hand to Rachel.

Ian had no time to be concerned. A speedboat shot past and at the same time that the wake hit, an unexpected gust smacked the cutter.

Unaware of the situation, Jeff laughed and gave Rachel a playful boost, coinciding with the boat's yaw and roll, sending the leeward rail toward the water.

Ian saw him stumble backward, and before Jeff could grab hold, he'd tumbled overboard. Esther let out a scream.

Rachel's frantic cry joined Esther's panic.

"Throw him the lifeline," Ian yelled, coming about and lifting a prayer to the Lord. He could wring Jeff's neck for his foolishness, but now it was too late. *Father, keep him safe.* The words soared heavenward with the increasing wind.

To Ian's grateful surprise, Esther had calmed herself and grabbed the tethered cushion. She hurled it overboard while Ian darted past her to drop the halyards.

"He went under," Rachel screamed. "He's drowning."

Ian glanced toward them.

"No," Esther yelled, "there he is. He's come up not too far from the cushion." She stood at the railing, extending the man-overboard pole.

"Swim," Rachel cried, clinging to the rail in tears. "Swim to the ladder."

"Calm down," Esther said, stretching her arms forward to reach him with the pole.

Esther called over her shoulder. "And we're drifting downwind toward him."

Ian hurried back to the wheel and came about while making a circle around Jeff as he floundered in the waves.

"He's got hold of it," Esther called.

Ian locked the wheel, then extracted the pole from Esther's clenched hands. When he looked over the rail, Jeff was clinging to the cushion, riding high on the growing rollers and paddling toward the boat while grinning at his predicament.

"Not funny," Ian muttered, reeling him in like a fish.

Jeff reached the ladder and hung there a moment, seeming to catch his breath. Finally he heaved himself up the rungs.

As Rachel leaned toward him as if to give him a hand, Ian let out a bellow. "Back off, Rachel."

She jumped back.

"If you're not careful, we'll have both of you in the water." Ian moved closer to hoist Jeff into the boat.

When he had both feet on the deck, Jeff stood in front of them with a grin plastered on his face and water running from his clothes. "Anyone else for a nice swim?"

Ian missed the humor. "Sit down, Jeff, before you fall overboard again. Esther, take the helm while I handle the sails. We need to get back. A storm's brewing."

Though fear now blanched her face, Esther stepped to the wheel and held the boat into the wind until he raised the sails and cleated the halyards.

"Everyone sit and don't move," Ian said, maneuvering himself back to the helm. "We've had enough excitement."

Looking at Esther, he knew he'd have a tough time getting her back on board for another sail. He clamped his jaw, not wanting to say any more to anyone.

After thanks and apologies, Rachel and Jeff headed to their car. Esther waited on board while Ian stowed the equipment. She hid her distress until after Jeff and Rachel had vanished beyond her line of vision, and then the thought of losing someone else from sailing blanketed her in anguish.

From the moment Jeff fell, her prayers had become a litany while she threw the cushion and played out the lifeline. She'd feared God would let her down, but the Lord had been merciful. Tangled in her distress, her heart filled with gratefulness.

Waiting for Ian, she sat on one of the cockpit settees, trembling and holding back the tears and frustration that knotted in her throat.

Anticipating an advancing storm, Ian hurried

around the deck, bagging the sails and stowing the gear. He worked with experience, and though frightened, Esther admired his competent, systematic action.

When the first drops of rain splatted against the deck, large icy drops hit Esther's bare arms and a chill rattled down her back.

"Go below," Ian called. "I'm almost finished."

She rose, opened the cabin door and climbed down the companionway. The sound of rain striking the cabin roof increased, and soon tears rolled down her cheeks as heavy as the rain.

"What's wrong?" Ian asked, dropping down the ladder and rushing to her side. The cabin door slammed behind him.

She shook her head, unable to speak and embarrassed with her excessive emotion.

Ian drew her against his damp shirt and enveloped her in his arms. Rainwater dripped from his hair and rolled down his face, but his body warmed her and gave her comfort.

"I'm sorry," she said hiccuping back a sob. "It was too much. Too frightening. Everything just hit me." She shook her head as if the motion would fling aside her anxiety and frustration.

"Relax," he said, running his hand down her back in soothing circles. "We're both upset."

Esther knew Ian had been disturbed by Jeff's foolish behavior. She'd never seen him that angry before, but she didn't blame him. She wanted to kick Jeff's immature rear. The picture disturbed her again.

Ian tilted up her chin and looked into her eyes.

"I'm so sorry this happened. If I could do it over, I'd tie Jeff to the mast. The whole thing was careless and pointless."

"It wasn't your fault, Ian."

He shifted his arm and pulled a handkerchief from his back pocket. With the tenderest look, he wiped the tears from her face. "I'm sorry. The hanky's wet from the rain."

"So are you," she said, pleased that a grin rose naturally on her mouth. Smiling felt good.

His fingers brushed against her cheek. "You look beautiful when you smile."

She shook her head. "I look horrible. I can imagine my raccoon eyes and pale face."

"But you're the prettiest raccoon I've ever met."

She saw it coming. A soft, tender look in his eyes all but melted her heart. His weighted eyelids closed and his lips lowered to meet hers with a touch so gentle, it could have been a dream.

But she knew it was real. The scent of citrus and rain-dampened cloth surrounded her as she clung to him, feeling rescued and protected.

He eased back, his eyes shrouded and filled with kindness.

Esther closed her eyes again and harnessed her longing. Ian felt sorry for her. That explained everything. Ian, the gentle giant out to save the forlorn maiden. She wondered how Jemma had missed his charm.

"Unless we're planning to wait out the storm, I suppose we should make a run for the car. Are you okay?"

She nodded, afraid to speak lest she give away the emotion he aroused in her. "I'm fine," she said, hearing her voice sound breathy but steady. "Let me fix my face. Okay?"

"Sure," he said, allowing her to slip from his arms.

She grabbed her bag and darted into the head. Before looking in the mirror, Esther splashed water on her face. When she inspected herself, she saw she'd been right. Her eyes were dark from her mascara, her hair tangled by the wind, but for a moment that didn't matter. Remembrance of the pressure of Ian's mouth against hers blocked out all other senses.

Her thoughts whirled, and she gripped the sink for support. What was she thinking? The whole thing was a game...a scheme to deceive her sister and Jeff. Instead, she'd fooled her own heart.

Chapter Eleven

Ian sat in the living room, studying Esther's father. He'd been surprised, expecting an older man for some reason. He guessed it was the man's old-fashioned philosophy.

Instead of a white-haired, stooped gentleman, Ian observed a man with graying hair, a straight back and a friendly twinkle in his eye. Though slightly paunchy, Uriah Downing looked in good physical condition.

"So tell me about this project you and my daughter are working on," he said.

"You'd find it boring, Mr. Downing," Ian said. An inviting aroma drifted in from the kitchen, and Ian felt his stomach gnaw with anticipation.

"Call me Uriah," her father said, "and let me decide for myself what I find boring."

His blunt response surprised Ian, and he covered his silent chuckle. Already Ian had seen a little of what Esther had said about him. Stubborn and decisive.

"I work for Bay Breeze Resort and—"

"What do you do there?"

"I'm the assistant manager," Ian said. "About the—"

"How does a job like that pay?" Uriah asked.

"Pay? It's a good living." Ian watched the expression on his face and realized Uriah was not a man to settle for a general statement. Ian spelled out dollars and cents, wondering if they would ever veer back to his original question.

Letting his gaze drift, Ian took in the living-room decor. Homey and neat, much like Esther's place. He noted a woman's touch in the room. Probably Esther's mother. A flowered print in the upholstery, a doily under the lamp. The house probably looked the same as it had the day she died.

"Sounds like you could take good care of a wife and family, then," Uriah said.

Ian's heart tripped over itself. Was he being interviewed as a prospective husband? "Yes, sir."

"Then why aren't you married?" The man leaned forward, his look direct and inquisitive.

His question unsettled Ian. Why wasn't he married? How could he answer that in fifty words or less?

"Don't tell me you're divorced," Uriah said, his back stiffening.

"No. No. I'm not divorced. I haven't married yet because God hasn't directed me to the right woman."

Uriah leaned back while a faint smile touched his face. "So you are a Christian."

"I am. Have been most of my life." Curious, Ian looked at the man. Why would Uriah have questioned it? Ian had been to church with them earlier that day. He'd sung the hymns and said the prayers.

"Most of your life?" He seemed to think that over a moment. "But when were you saved?"

Ian wondered where Uriah kept his interrogation lights. If this weren't a grilling, he didn't know what was. "I was saved when Jesus died on the cross." He watched Uriah's eyes narrow. "But if you mean when did I make my faith public, I was a young teenager."

Uriah's eyes widened and he nodded. "Good."

Ian let out a pent-up breath and relaxed his shoulders.

"You know," Uriah said, "sometimes young men hang around my daughters claiming to be Christians, but I can usually spot the ones who aren't."

Tension traveled up Ian's back. He longed to ask Uriah if he'd passed his scrutinizing or not, but common sense urged him to keep quiet.

"I'd say you're an honest Christian."

"Thank you," Ian said, wishing now they could get back to Bay Breeze. That topic, boring or not, seemed safer.

"Time to eat," Esther called from the doorway.

Ian wanted to leap up and kiss her for the reprieve. He held himself back, waiting for Uriah to make the first move. He didn't want to look overenthusiastic.

Esther's father braced himself on the armrest and

pushed himself up. "Bad knees," he said to Ian. "I had to retire early. Couldn't work any longer."

"What did you do?" Ian asked, rising and following him toward the mouthwatering aroma.

"Plumber. Took care of people's drains." He glanced at Ian over his shoulder. "You can learn a lot about people that way."

Looking down pipes? Ian wondered what Uriah could learn about him if he started checking out his drains? "That's interesting."

"Daddy," Esther said, rolling her eyes. She gestured toward a chair before heading through another doorway.

Ian sat where she'd indicated, at the end of the oblong table across from her father. Noticing Uriah's chair had arms, Ian wondered if it was to help him stand when they'd finished the meal or perhaps to allow him to feel more in charge...like at a board meeting. Ian cringed at his snide thought.

Esther returned, carrying a large platter of pot roast circled by oven-browned potatoes and carrots. The fragrance filled the room while Ian's hunger grew. A tossed salad and rolls were also on the table for them. Ian hadn't had a home-cooked meal this elegant in years.

Esther sat on the side between them and extended her hands in both directions.

Ian took her hand and, realizing they were about to say the blessing, bowed his head.

Uriah cleared his throat and began. "Heavenly Father, we want to praise You and thank You for all You give us each day. We thank You for this wonderful meal cooked by my eldest daughter, a young woman who needs Your blessings, Lord. We just want You to know that her life needs to be fulfilled.''

Esther's hand tensed in his, and Ian peeked with one eye, wanting to see her face. Her eyes were squeezed closed and he could almost hear the *amen* she wanted to assert.

''And we give You thanks for company. A good Christian man who's been blessed with a steady job and a good income. Lord, just give him what he needs to make him feel complete.''

Ian knew what Uriah had in mind, and if Ian had anything to do with it, he would make Uriah a very happy man. He pushed away his grin.

''In Jesus' precious name we pray. Amen.''

At Uriah's *amen,* Ian and Esther echoed their own. Ian opened his eyes and watched a pink flush climb up Esther's neck. She offered him the roast without looking into his eyes. Ian filled his plate and passed the dish to her father.

''Now, let's get back to that project,'' Uriah said, dipping a roll into his gravy.

Ian thought Uriah had long forgotten Bay Breeze, but he used the topic to include Esther in the conversation. They took turns. While one chewed, the other told her father about the research. Ian felt certain Esther had already told him everything, but he proved to be a determined man.

Into a second helping, Uriah settled back against his chair and eyed Ian. ''Then you must know Jeff Langley.''

''Yes, I do.''

Uriah propped an elbow on the table and leaned forward. "What do you think of him?"

Ian's meal did a double axel, followed by a triple lutz. Esther's father knew how to put a man on the spot.

"Daddy, please don't ask—"

"Let the man answer, Esther."

Ian's moment of respite sank to his toes. "He's on time and knows his job." That seemed safe and truthful.

"Do you think he's a Christian?" Uriah asked.

This answer was easy. "We've never talked about our faith, so I don't know."

"You've never witnessed to him?" His eyebrows arched upward.

Wanting to kick himself, Ian searched for an appropriate answer. "Our paths don't cross too often, and when they do, we talk about the resort needs. He's honest and helpful, though. I'd suspect he's a believer."

Uriah nodded. "Me, too." He pursed his lips as he lifted his knife, slivered off a hunk of roast and speared it. "But I think he needs to grow up." He used his fork as a pointer.

"Don't overeat, Daddy. I have dessert," Esther said.

Ian wondered if the dessert would lodge in his throat like the excellent dinner that he'd hoped to enjoy.

Uriah ignored her and continued to aim the fork at Ian. "He wants to marry my daughter Rachel."

Ian pondered if he should admit he knew, or not

respond. He glanced at Esther and sensed he should be truthful. "Yes. Esther told me."

"What do you think about that, Ian?" Uriah's casual look didn't match the intrigue reflected in his eyes.

"I'm not sure I understand your question, Uriah. Rachel and Jeff are a young couple who've fallen in love. So I guess the natural desire would be to get married."

"But you said the key word. Young."

"They're voting age," Ian said, then wished he hadn't. What did voting have to do with marriage? He waited for Uriah to ask the same question.

"That doesn't mean he has the wisdom to vote." Uriah shoveled in a mouthful of potatoes.

Ian had lost his appetite long ago.

Esther's shoulders rose, and she came to his rescue, repeating what Ian already knew. "My dad believes that I should marry before my sister, Ian. That's what bothers him."

"Oh." He looked from Esther to Uriah, wondering what to say.

"If the girls' mother was here," Uriah said, "she and I could talk about this. Marge was tuned in to the Lord. She had the wisdom of Solomon...but she's gone. Now I'm left trying to be a wise father." He shook his head. "The Lord could have granted me a few more years with Marge, but He must have needed her in heaven."

"You've been a wonderful father," Esther said, patting his hand. "We just have a different belief than you do about that issue, Dad. That's all." She glanced at Ian. "But don't ask Ian to get involved in our difference of opinion. You're making both of us uncomfortable."

"Really?" A frown crossed Uriah's features. "I thought we were just sharing beliefs." He studied Ian with a hopeful look.

"If you want my opinion," Ian said, hoping he could help and not hinder the situation, "I'm a New Testament man myself. I think when the Lord directs a man and woman to fall in love and they want to marry, who am I to interfere in the Lord's doing?"

Uriah pinched his lips together and stared at the tablecloth.

Ian's heart rose to his throat, and he gave Esther a quick look.

She shrugged, apparently as puzzled as he was about how her father would react.

Finally Uriah looked at them. "That's something to pray about, Ian."

Esther breathed a deep sigh, grateful to Ian for his comment. Her dad had taken it well, and maybe hearing it from someone else—especially another man— he'd give it some thought "Who'd like dessert?" she asked, changing the subject. She rose and began stacking the dishes.

"She makes good pie," Uriah said, giving Ian a wink.

"I'll have a piece," Ian said.

"Make that two…and coffee." Uriah held up two fingers.

Esther grabbed the platter and salad, then headed for the kitchen. Standing alone, she drew in a calming breath. She felt terrible having put Ian through this, but now he'd met her father and perhaps would better understand. Her dad had done the best he could. Esther loved him and honored him, even though it was difficult. That's all that was important.

She pushed the button on the coffeemaker before cutting the pie. She'd baked the pie and brought it to her father's last night after the sailing fiasco. It had been her way of distracting herself, rather than sitting home and wondering what to do.

Ian's unexpected kiss had kept her awake all night. The memory of his arms wrapped around her, his tender lips on hers sent Esther's mind heading into places it shouldn't go.

Ian had been wonderful. Helpful on the project and a trouper at trying to divert Rachel's attention, but the whole thing had been based on deception. No matter how she looked at it.

During the worship service that morning, she'd been stunned by the guilt that raked over her. In her attempt to get Rachel off her back, she'd let her sister believe that she and Ian were a couple. That they were falling in love and that marriage was a possibility. Utter deceit. And deceit was a sin.

She needed the courage to tell Rachel the truth and to drop the game she and Ian were playing. Or she could take the coward's way out by asking God's forgiveness and telling Ian the scam had ended. At least Rachel would give up on her hopeless dreams.

As the thought rifled through her, loneliness raced along her spine and weighed upon her heart. She'd miss Ian more than she could say. He'd brought adventure to her life and filled her quiet nights with good talk and camaraderie. Even the charade, as sinful as it was, had given her pleasure—holding his hand, feeling safe in his arms and enjoying the touch of his lips. She longed for it all to be real.

Guaranteed, they'd formed a true friendship, bonded by mutual respect and faith. Even though he'd never be hers for real, she liked him.

The gurgle of the coffeemaker pulled her back to her task. Esther placed the plates, cups and pot on a large tray and headed for the dining room.

Soft laughter met her ears when she came through the doorway, and she eyed both men, realizing they were deep in conversation. When she set the tray on the table, Ian looked up and smiled.

"Your dad was telling me some plumbing tales. Pretty funny stuff."

"Not all of it's funny," Uriah said, "but we can all use a good laugh now and again."

"Sure can," Ian said, accepting the plate she offered. "Looks good, Esther." He eyed the pie as if trying to see what it was.

"Elderberry," she said. "Dad's favorite." She handed her father a piece, then hesitated. "I saw some ice cream in the freezer. Who'd like some?"

Two hands jutted into the air, and she retraced her steps, returning with the carton. With the coffee served, she sat down and picked up her fork.

"So what's next on the research?" her father asked.

"Esther and I are going to White Lake next week. We want to visit a sailing excursion company."

Esther's stomach tightened. She'd forgotten. They'd be spending another full day together. Her emotions wavered like a swing in the wind. She loved being together and hated it at the same time.

"Good idea talking to the horse's mouth," her dad said, a twinkle in his eye. "Talk with someone who knows."

Someone who knows. God knew everything. Esther concentrated on the pie while her mind raced for decisions. She needed to spend time with the Lord. She wanted to know her heart...and what her heavenly Father had planned for her.

Lifting her eyes, she watched her dad and Ian chatter together—the two most important men in her life.

Chapter Twelve

Ian looked through the window at the line of sail-boats docked in the small marina, then back to the owner of White Lake Sailing Adventures. "You've been very helpful." He glanced at Esther's notepad filled with a multitude of information. "I think you've answered just about all of our questions."

"Would you like to take a closer look?" Wes Garrison asked. "I can tell you a little about the boats we're using and which ones I'd recommend."

"What do you think?" Ian asked, making sure Esther wanted to take the time.

She nodded, folding the notebook and slipping it into her pocket.

Garrison stepped to the door and opened it, motioning for them to follow.

Stepping into the sun, Ian inhaled the fresh lake air. Being on the water surrounded by sailboats gave him the urge to hurry back to Loving and sail his cutter. The season would draw to a close soon.

Out on the pier, Ian grasped Esther's arm as they walked along the rough planks. If recommendations were to be made, he thought Esther would want to suggest the most useful and practical vessels for the resort. Looking at the boats and getting Garrison's opinions seemed worth the time.

Their footsteps thudded on the boards, and looking down at the pier, Ian noticed Esther had worn practical shoes with rubber soles. He grinned, thinking of her expression the day he'd suggested they walk along the shore when she had worn dress shoes.

Garrison paused. "Now, here's one I'd recommend. This is a forty-foot ketch," he said, gesturing to one of the larger vessels. "It's great for a full day on the lake. The cabin is roomy with a large dinette, a settee and a workable galley."

"Looks like it could sleep about eight people," Ian said.

"Right. It has two heads with showers. We added a bimini strong enough for sunbathing or for sitting. Even a place to pack the sails."

"I've never heard of a hardtop bimini," Ian said. "Aren't they usually cloth?"

"This one's specially made," Garrison said.

"It's a beauty." Ian looked at it with longing, already dreaming of buying a bigger boat someday.

"It carries five hundred gallons of water and a thousand of fuel."

Impressed, Ian nodded. If he had a sailboat this large he could spend a week or more exploring quaint ports and exotic islands.

"Look back here," Garrison said, motioning them

to the stern. "We added this four-foot swim platform and ladder. Easy access to water."

"That's a great feature," Esther added, pulling out her notebook and making notations. "That and the bimini."

He beckoned them along, and as they went, Garrison pointed out a smaller sloop, probably thirty-four feet, excellent for a few hours' sailing, and another ketch suitable for three or four sailors who wanted to experience an overnight trip.

When Garrison had finished, they followed him back to the building. Ian's mind felt saturated with information, and he was pleased that Esther had picked up brochures and taken volumes of notes—the model and details of each vessel. They could discuss them all later.

"Thanks for your help," Ian said, extending his hand to the owner.

Garrison grasped it. "You're welcome. If you think of anything later, feel free to call."

"I may just do that," Esther said, thanking him before they left.

With their Sailing Adventures brochures and the notebook, Ian and Esther headed to his car. In the parking lot the gravel crunched beneath their feet and the seagulls wheeled overhead, filling the air with their raucous cries. Ian opened Esther's door, and when she was seated, he rounded the car and climbed inside.

"My mind's loaded," he said, taking a long, slow look at Esther's face. She'd been quiet today. More businesslike.

Wishing he knew why, Ian reviewed the past Sunday when he'd met her father. Ian had thought the day had gone well...at least for Rachel and Jeff. Uriah had said he'd pray about Ian's way of looking at the situation, and that seemed like a good step to Ian.

Esther leaned over and slid the booklets and note-pad into an attaché case before turning to face him. "I thought this was worthwhile. Thanks for your help."

"You're welcome," he said, sensing again the distance between them. Knowing if he let things go they would only get worse, he grappled for a solution. "I'm starving," he said, hoping a lunch outing would also break the tension. "Let's stop and eat."

"That's fine," she said.

"How about the Crosswinds? They have good food."

"Sure. Anything," she said.

Her response seemed lackluster, but he didn't let that sway him. They traveled the short distance in silence, and after he parked, Ian hurried around to open her door.

"Thanks," she said, stepping to the pavement. She walked beside him into the restaurant.

The dining room was quiet. Only a few tables were filled and the guests were widely spaced around the room, allowing customers some privacy. Ian held Esther's chair until she was seated, then slid onto another. In unison, they lifted the menus and surveyed the choices.

When Ian made his selection, he placed the menu on the table corner, folded his hands and waited.

After a lengthy pause, Esther looked up. ''You've decided already?'' she asked.

He gave her a slight nod, returning her silence.

She shot him a knowing look as if she realized he was echoing her withdrawal. Placing her menu on top of his, she gave him a direct look. ''I'm making better progress than I'd expected on the research. I may have it ready sooner than the first of the year.''

The announcement surprised him—disappointed him, in a way. ''Philip will appreciate that,'' he said. Though the conversation had only turned to Bay Breeze, Ian felt grateful they were talking.

''I'll go over the information with you beforehand,'' she said, ''but I think Philip's wasting his time with any consideration of acquiring fishing charters.''

''Why's that?'' Ian asked.

''Too many companies in the area. Over thirty, if I remember correctly.''

''That many?''

She nodded. ''It would hardly be worth the cost of a captain and crew. Let alone the boat, gear and insurance.''

''I really thought having a fishing charter available at the resort would be a nice draw for guests,'' Ian said. ''Better than having to arrange their own bookings in advance.''

She straightened. ''But I have an idea. I even sent out a couple of feelers.''

She'd piqued his interest.

Esther sipped the glass of water before continuing. "What do you think about negotiating a contract with a nearby fishing charter company?"

"What do you mean—contract?" Ian asked.

Her face brightened and her voice rose with enthusiasm. "Bay Breeze could work out a deal with a nearby fishing charter. The resort would bring them new business, and in return, the resort guests would get a discount."

Amazed at her creative idea, Ian reached across and rested his palm on her hand. "That's good thinking, Esther." Even the simple touch sent longing scurrying through his chest.

"The typical fee is about a hundred dollars plus another hundred per hour. So four hours costs about $495. If the charter company would knock off a hundred, let's say, that would be a saving to resort guests and no great loss to the charter company." Her voice died away.

Ian glanced over his shoulder and spotted the waitress, and they curbed their conversation until she took their orders and picked up the menus.

When she left, Ian continued. "Did you say you'd put out some feelers?"

Esther nodded. "Two of the four companies I spoke with sounded like they'd be willing to negotiate. Philip might work toward a bigger discount, but anything would help."

Ian agreed, and seeing her enthusiasm made him even happier.

Their food arrived, and during the meal they rehashed the sailboats and what might work for Bay

Breeze. Ian agreed the boats would be a great draw, and he felt confident that Philip would want to add at least one, maybe two vessels to be available to the resort guests for a fee.

He finished his sandwich first and leaned back, sipping his soda and watching Esther take bites of her taco salad. She picked up a corn chip and nibbled on it, then used another to scoop up some of the meat sauce. She mesmerized him.

When Ian first met Esther, she'd come across as authoritative, intelligent and decisive. Now he observed her vulnerability, the part of her she hid from most people by not getting too familiar with them.

But he'd gotten close to her—closer than most, he guessed—and her sensitive side nudged Ian's heart. She was as tough as cotton...and as pure.

"Why are you looking at me?" Esther asked.

Uneasy that she'd noticed, Ian chuckled. "Just thinking about us."

A frown narrowed her eyes, and tension pulled at her mouth. "What do you mean, us?"

"How well we've gotten to know each other," he said. "I understand everyone keeps part of his psyche a secret, but..." He hesitated, not knowing how to say what he was thinking without Esther building her protective wall. "We've become real friends."

She didn't move, instead studied his face.

Ian held his breath, wondering what was coming.

Her eyes shifted. "Yes. We have become friends."

He relaxed and filled his lungs.

"But...I suppose that's the problem."

"Problem?" Ian faltered. Only Esther could find difficulty with having a friendship. His shoulders drooped while he waited.

A misty glaze filled her eyes, and he noticed her cheek tremble. "I feel guilty. Sitting in church last Sunday, everything hit me. The deceit. The injury. The sin."

"Whoa." Ian straightened his back and lost any sense of good humor. "We created a little cover-up to give you a break from Rachel's matchmaking. Most of the assumption was part of Rachel's and Jeff's imaginations."

That wasn't exactly true. The relationship had become real to Ian. Only Esther fought getting close and letting go of her single life.

"But we did things to lead them on. You can't deny that." Her misty eyes widened.

"At first, yes. I admit that, but then we reacted with real emotions, Emotions of two people who'd…become friends." He'd almost slipped and said two people who loved each other. He couldn't deceive himself anymore. Telling her—no matter what happened—was all he could do.

He grasped his courage. "Esther, listen—"

"No, you listen, Ian. Yes, you've been a…good friend. I enjoy your company, but you and I both know we have absolutely no intention of making any more of this relationship than what it is. A friendship."

His lips twitched with the words he'd started to say. Maybe she knew that she had no intention, but Ian had begun to feel differently. Much differently.

His admiration had grown. His enjoyment of her company had grown. His yearning for a loving commitment with her had grown.

Her words catapulted from his head to his heart. Why make a fool of himself, falling on his knees and begging her to love him? Better rise to the occasion and agree. "Okay." His chest ached with the pounding of his heart. "So what are you…we going to do?"

"You don't have to do anything. I can tell her we broke up," Esther said, a look of sadness filling her eyes.

"But that's more deceit," he said, hoping to help her come to her senses. "Let's just let things go, Esther, and see what happens."

He grasped her hand, yearning to bring it to his lips and kiss it. "Your father's thinking over what I said. Remember? He said he'd pray about it. If God's willing, he may just change his mind. Then the point is moot. Why upset Rachel if there's no need?"

Praying she'd listen, Ian watched her expression shift and change.

"You've made a point, but…" She lowered her head and lifted her hand, stroking the bridge of her nose. "But if this gets out of hand any more than it already has, I'll have to talk with Rachel and tell her it was all a game."

The whole thing had begun as a charade for Esther, but not for Ian. He couldn't tell her now. His feelings for her had germinated for a year before he'd initiated any real contact, thinking it might blossom into a meaningful relationship. "Whatever you have to do."

Her look settled the matter. She'd ended it, and he would keep quiet. "When should we get together to go over this part of the report?"

She pushed her salad away, half-uneaten, wiped the napkin across her mouth and dropped it on the table. "Give me a few weeks."

He only nodded, his mind heavy with thought. Silence stretched into discomfort. "Dessert?"

"No," she said.

"Then we can go." He pushed back his chair and rose. Before he could get to Esther she had swiveled in her chair and was standing.

He still had time. Time to capture Esther's heart. Time to test his courage and tell her the truth.

"What do you think?" Esther asked, shifting her focus from the report.

"Perfect." Ian held a copy in his hand and fingered the pages. "Philip will be impressed, and I think you've come to a perfect conclusion. One sailboat the first year, then another if it looks successful, and work out a contract with a local fishing charter. You get an A plus."

"Thanks." She sent him a sincere smile.

"I'll set up an appointment with Philip so you can do an oral presentation."

"That's good," she said. "Once he's had a chance to read it, I'll answer any questions."

"It's a good report. I know he'll think it's money well spent."

"I couldn't have done it without you. I think you know that," Esther said.

"Yes, you could," he said. He paused a moment, then let the conversation shift in another direction. "Any news from your dad?"

"News?"

"Has he said anything about changing his mind? Blessing Rachel and Jeff's engagement?"

Esther shook her head. "God will have to hit him with a club."

A chuckle flew from Ian before he could contain it. "Sorry, but that struck me funny."

"Funny, but true. Dad's probably still praying." She rubbed the back of her neck. "I told Rachel that you'd met Dad and what you'd said. She was thrilled and hopeful." She let her hand drop to her lap. "That's the part that bothers me."

"You mean being hopeful?"

"Yes. I told her not to get too excited about it all, but Rachel's backed in a corner. She loves Dad, and naturally she loves Jeff. Which one will she hurt? It's a no-win situation."

"Being an optimistic sort, I'd like to think your dad will eventually come around."

She released a faint chuckle. "I'd like to think the same, but like I said, God will have to use a club. No matter. You made a valiant effort." The good humor stayed on her face.

Feeling assured, Ian rose and walked to the edge of her desk. He leaned against it and lifted her hand from the report. "These fingers have worked so hard.

What do you think about giving them a break and having dinner with me tonight?"

Her smile faded. "I can't, Ian, but thanks. I promised Rachel I'd go with her to the Grand Haven Streetfest."

Ian tried to cover his disappointment. "Where's Jeff?"

"He's working overtime tonight. Someone's ill. But he said he'd have a replacement in a few hours and meet her there later."

"Would you mind if I came along?" Ian asked, grasping his courage. He'd put her on the spot, but at this point, all seemed fair in love and war.

Pausing, she slipped her hand from his, then rolled back the chair to rise. "I don't see why not. We can eat junk food there. Maybe some of those sausages you love."

Ian shifted from the edge of her desk, pleased she remembered. "Do you want to call Rachel to warn her?"

"Warn her?"

"That I'm coming along."

She sent him a faint smile. "No, she won't care."

"What about Rachel's sister?"

Esther eyed him a moment as if she didn't understand. Finally his question sank in and she laughed. "She doesn't mind at all."

Grinning, he unloosened his arm and darted

Chapter Thirteen

Esther hid the excitement she felt with Ian at her side. Last year she'd come to the city's annual Streetfest alone, ambling along Washington Avenue and feeling like an outsider from the world.

Tonight after Rachel and Jeff found each other, she and Ian meandered down the sidewalk, gawking at all the stands and displays. The city's autumn tradition brought the community downtown to enjoy dinner at one of the restaurants or fill up at the stands providing food samples, to visit the merchants' exhibits and to dance in the street until midnight.

When the crowd became heavy, Ian slid his arm around her back, maneuvering her through the groups of window-shoppers and around the food displays. "There's cider over there. Want some?"

"Sure. It'll help wash down the crackers and spicy cheese spread," Esther said, reiterating the storekeeper's pitch.

Grinning, he unloosened his arm and darted to the

local cider mill display. He hurried back with two small paper cups. "Only a mouthful, but it's better than nothing."

She took a sip, enjoying the cleansing tang that helped to quench her thirst. "I should buy a jug before I leave tonight."

"See, these displays aren't here for nothing," he said, downing the contents of his cup in one swallow.

Two more sips and hers vanished. She crinkled the paper and tossed it into a trash can. "Couldn't ask for a nicer evening." Beneath the aroma of food, the scent of autumn hung on the air—drying leaves and moldering earth bound in a crisp breeze from the north.

"Problem is," he said, "it means winter's on the way. I like the autumn colors, but I miss summer."

She smiled. "It's the boating you miss."

"You know me best," he said, and gave her arm a squeeze. "I'd like to take the boat out at least once more before I have to put it in storage."

Esther heard it coming and prepared herself.

"I know your last trip was so awful. Terrible memories instead of the good ones I'd hoped you'd have."

He paused, and she waited.

"I hoped you might come with me again. Give it another try."

She shook her head. "That's what I'm afraid of."

"Seriously. It'll be our celebration…finishing the report early. Please. Come with me?"

"Oh, Ian—"

"I know, Esther, but you were handling it, and I really think you should give it one more try."

"Why?"

"Because."

His abrupt answer tickled her, and she laughed. "How can a woman say no with an explanation like that?"

He slipped his arm around her waist. "When it comes to words, I'm prolific."

They reached the end of the street, close to the lake. On a temporary platform a local band had just returned from their break and struck up a loud rock-and-roll tune. The thrumming bass notes reverberated through the air, and couples left sidewalk attractions to dance on the street.

"Be honest, and tell me if I ever look like that," Ian yelled above the noise.

She didn't bother to respond. Her voice would have been lost in the wailing arpeggio of the lead guitar. Though Esther loved the rhythm and beat of a good band, her preference leaned toward something soft and mellow. Still, tonight she couldn't help but tap her foot.

When the song ended, Ian leaned closer. "Let's hope the next one's a little softer."

"I second that motion," she said.

His wish came true. The guitars muted, and a singer stepped to the mike, sending out the words to a popular love song.

"Dance?" Ian asked.

Her heart skipped. "I haven't danced in years."

She hadn't been kidding when she said years. Probably high school.

He didn't accept her excuse. "Just follow me," he said, taking her hand and luring her into the street.

Slipping his arm around her back, Ian tucked her hand against his chest and guided her into the rhythm.

Esther fell into step, and when she calmed, she sensed he did, too, swaying and pivoting to the music and tempting her to stay in his embrace forever. She inched her hand along his arm, enjoying the feel of his hard muscles tensing and easing beneath his lightweight jacket. He rested his cheek against her hair, and she basked in the warmth and closeness of his body.

When the music stopped, Esther pivoted toward the sidewalk, positive the next song would be another raucous tune, but instead, the band swayed into another sweet song.

Ian didn't let her escape, but drew her even closer to his chest. She looked into his eyes, and seeing his smile sent her heart skittering.

"Having fun?" he asked.

Afraid to speak, she nodded.

In the distance she caught a glimpse of Rachel and Jeff clinging to each other like two lovesick teens. Esther's heart flooded with sadness, and she wished her father would relent.

When she tensed, Ian seemed to notice and he shifted his head in her sister's direction. He turned back and gave her gentle smile. "Have faith. God will work everything out."

God will work everything out. If only she had Ian's confidence.

He nuzzled her cheek, and she closed her eyes, loving every moment yet fearing the future. What would she do when the charade ended?

Esther yearned to be his friend, but she'd left the realms of friendship long ago. Her feelings had blossomed and grown to something sweeter and more lasting, and though Ian treated her with kindness, she sensed he had no intentions concerning anything other than what they'd stated—a silly scheme. Ian seemed to enjoy the fantasy.

The lazy melody drifted to an end, yet Ian held her fast, swaying to imaginary music. She would have stayed there for hours, if she could, wrapped in contentment.

When he slowed, then stopped, Esther looked into his face and regarded Ian's mouth descending to hers. She wanted to step back, to stop his lips from caressing hers, but she lost the inner battle. Instead, she tiptoed to meet his soft mouth and languish in the tender touch of his lips.

After she eased away, confusion and pleasure battled in her heart. "Why—wh—what happened?"

"I kissed you."

"I know, but I mean…why? Were Rachel and Jeff watching us or…?" She didn't know what she meant, but she wanted to understand why he'd kissed her so sweetly.

"Sure," he said.

"Oh," was all she could say, disappointed that the kiss had only been part of the scheme.

* * *

Hearing the knocking, Esther slipped into her denim slacks and hurried toward the door. Ian couldn't be there already, she was sure. He'd said eleven, and it was only a little after ten.

She pulled open the door and saw Rachel standing on the driveway, her face pale, her eyes red rimmed.

"What's wrong?" Esther pushed open the door and stepped back.

Rachel marched inside, headed for the living room and caved into a chair. "I'm so frustrated I could scream."

"About what? Is it Jeff again?"

"Him, too," Rachel said, "but it's Dad. Nothing has changed except he admits he was wrong."

"Dad?" Esther's body straightened with the news. If it was true, then Rachel's distress seemed inappropriate. She should be leaping for joy. "Did I hear you say Dad admitted he was wrong?"

Rachel nodded. "He did, but he said it didn't matter."

Esther's happiness spiraled into confusion.

"Dad thought that out of respect for you—being the oldest—I should wait until you're engaged before Jeff and I can talk about marriage. I hope Ian's about ready to ask you."

Esther's shoulders drooped and her legs buckled beneath her, sending her quaking body to the sofa. "Rachel, it's useless."

"Why? What do you mean?"

The guilt of Esther's deceit rose in full fury. "I'm not going to be engaged. Ever." She ran her hand across her face and covered her mouth as reality struck her with force. Rachel needed to know the truth.

Rachel slid to the edge of her seat. "But what about you and—"

"It's a charade. We have no relationship. We did it so that you'd get off my back about dating."

Rachel's face blanched the color of new snow. "You can't mean this."

Sorrow flooded Esther. "But I do."

"No, Esther. You two look so...so good together. I know I've seen a special spark between you. You can't be serious." Rachel's hands quivered as she ran them along her throat.

"I'm so sorry. It started out as a way to keep you and Jeff from manipulating my life. We should have ended the ruse long ago."

Rachel's blank stare sent ice through Esther's veins, but she continued. "Ian and I had to work together on the project...so we just let you think..." Tears welled in her eyes as she saw her sister's heartbreak. "I do like Ian. A lot. But it's one-sided. Nothing will come of it. So stop hoping."

"I should be angry at you," Rachel said. "I should get up and walk out of here, but I can't." She lowered her head to her lap, then lifted it. "Jeff and I were wrong to play matchmaker. I knew it when I agreed."

"I know," Esther said.

"But what will I do now, Esther? How can I tell Jeff that Dad's sticking to the whole thing even though he knows he's wrong? It doesn't make sense.''

Esther agreed with that. It made no sense at all. ''I'll talk to him tonight. At least I can be truthful with him now.''

''He really likes Ian,'' Rachel mumbled. ''I think seeing you two together gave him confidence that you would...'' Her voice faded in defeat.

Her father's attitude struck an unpleasant chord, and Esther's anger grew. ''I'll tell you what I just realized,'' she said, her voice sparking with indignation. ''I thought this was like old times. I had to do everything first. But this is different. Dad's been matchmaking in his own way, Rachel. He's as bad as you and Jeff.''

She rose and paced the floor. ''He wants both his daughters married and cared for, so to make sure it happened, he insisted you wait until I married. See. It puts pressure on me—who'd been happy and content as a single person—to find someone, so *you* can be happy.'' She slammed her hand against the doorjamb. ''He's done it all our lives.''

''Do you really think he did that?'' Rachel asked.

Esther clamped her hands into fists. ''Do I think? I know. Can't you see it?''

''What will we do? What will *I* do?'' Rachel asked, rising and crossing to Esther. She lifted her arms and wrapped them around Esther's neck.

''I can't think right now,'' Esther said. ''I'm leaving in a few minutes. I have plans.'' She avoided mentioning Ian. His name would only stir up expectations. More hopes. "But I'll see Dad tonight like I said. I'm upset, but I'll think of something."

Rachel's arms slid from their embrace and hung at her side while her eyes narrowed and her mouth pinched with thought. "Something's just struck me. Something important."

Esther's pulse tripped as she watched her sister's face. "What is it?"

"God's telling us something, Esther. I feel it." She grasped Esther's shoulders. "I've been fighting the Lord and manipulating you. I'm frustrated with Dad. It's not right."

Imagining what Rachel had in mind, Esther's stomach churned with concern.

"I'm putting everything in God's hands. That's all I can do," Rachel said. "If Jeff loves me—really loves me—he'll pray with me and let God's will be done. Maybe our marriage isn't meant to be." Though she said the words, tears welled in her eyes.

"Don't do anything rash," Esther said. "I'll be gone all afternoon, but we can talk when I get back. Is that okay?"

Rachel nodded. "I feel better already. Pray with me before I go. Okay?"

Her heart fluttering in her chest, Esther grasped Rachel's hands as they prayed.

Ian's hands faltered as he raised the sails then settled back in the cockpit. Esther seemed thoughtful, but she acted calmer than he'd seen her in months. Maybe ever. He wondered what had caused the change. Whatever had generated it, he felt grateful.

Sailing had a romantic allure for many people. To-day Ian had chosen the setting for his own purpose, a purpose he'd tossed around in his mind for the past weeks ever since he'd known for certain he loved Esther.

"Want a soda?" Esther asked, sitting nearby on a bench.

"Sounds good," he said, watching her rise and grab the door to make her way down to the cabin. Her windbreaker rustled in the crisp breeze. He hoped she'd be warm enough. If not, his arms would do the trick.

His thoughts drifted back to the Streetfest. The im-age of holding Esther in his arms, her petite frame so close he could feel her breath against his cheek, sent longing skipping through his chest. When they'd first stepped into the street she'd tensed as he swayed to the music, but in a heartbeat her body had moved with his, slow and easy like the sailboat on a still summer afternoon.

Esther had become his summer. His sailboat. His dream. No longer could he play this game, pretend-ing it was only a make-believe romance.

Esther appeared in the companionway, carrying two sodas and with a bag of potato chips tucked un-der her arm. "Thought you might like a snack," she said, handing him a soft drink.

She set hers on the bench and tore open the chip bag, extending it toward him.

He patted the seat beside him. "Only if you sit here. We can share."

The sun drifted behind a cloud, and a gust of

colder wind whipped through the sails. Esther shivered with the chill. "And you can block the icy air." She sat beside him, propping the sack on her thigh.

He plunged his hand into the bag and pulled out a handful, maneuvering a few to his mouth. Crumbs fell and sailed away on the breeze.

They sat in silence, munching and drinking soda. With each gust, Esther nestled against him, using him as a barricade.

When the cloud drifted and the sun brightened the sky, Esther straightened. "That feels good."

"This is why I store the boat at the end of September. We might have a few warm days, but out here it gets cold." He struggled with himself, wondering about the best time to initiate his confession.

"I'm feeling better today," she said, standing a moment to look out at the sun-sprinkled ripples. "You guessed the truth when we first met. I did miss sailing, but the fear paralyzed me. Little by little, I hope I feel more confident."

"You will," he agreed. "The more positive experiences you have, the more your anxiety will fade." The words had deeper meaning for him. His feelings for Esther had secured themselves in his heart.

He tugged on the hem of her jacket. When she looked at him, he pointed to the seat and extended his arm for her to nestle beside him.

She grinned and sat in his embrace. "I know. And I can give my fears to God." She paused, then added, "I hate to put a damper on today," she said, "but I had another unpleasant half hour with Rachel before you came.''

''That's too bad.'' He'd sensed something had happened, but no matter how unpleasant, he knew she'd gained a new resolve. Something had calmed her.

She told him what had happened—her father's admission of wrong-thinking, but his determination to remain unchanged.

''We prayed,'' Esther finished, ''and I felt covered by a reassuring calm. I realized that God's in charge. I can't force things in my own direction, and neither can Rachel. It's a simple concept, but one we Christians have a hard time accepting.''

Ian nodded. ''I know exactly what you mean. I ask God for guidance, and then I strike out on my own, never waiting to listen.''

''We are stubborn children, aren't we?'' Esther said.

She quieted again, the only sound the splash of the water against the hull and an occasional cry of a seagull overhead. When Esther lifted her head, Ian saw a different look in her eyes. ''As I prayed with Rachel, I asked God for forgiveness.'' She shifted her body to face him. ''I talked with her, Ian. I don't want to ruin one of your last days out here on the lake, but I told Rachel about our charade.''

His pulse quickened as alarm trickled down his back. ''How did she take it?''

''Better than I expected.''

''She wasn't angry?''

Esther shrugged. ''I think she was hurt more than

angry. But she did have a revelation. We'd upset each other trying to maneuver our own lives." She ran her hand along the back of her neck. "Now I don't know what will happen with Jeff."

"You mean when she tells him?"

"When she tells him she's not doing anything without God's direction."

Ian understood her concern. Jeff didn't seem the type who had a close relationship with the Lord. He was a believer, Ian was sure, but his rash, hyperactive spirit didn't make him seem like one who'd wait on God's bidding. "I can see why you're concerned," he said, realizing the conversation had set up the perfect opening for his confession.

Adjusting the sail into the wind, he felt the boat slow as the wind left the mainsail with a snap and flutter. He shifted to face her more directly and took her hand.

Seeming surprised, she jerked her head upward and a look of confusion settled on her face.

"I might have a solution for this whole situation," Ian said, hoping his timing had been directed by the Lord and was not another of his own bad decisions.

"A solution?"

Chapter Fourteen

Esther's eyes widened in seeming disbelief. "What do you mean?"

Ian swallowed, ready to admit the truth. "The day I suggested you let Rachel think we were dating...well, I did it for a more selfish reason."

Her perplexity shifted to a scowl. "What reason?"

"I'd always admired you, Esther. My visits to the library were sometimes motivated more by talking with you than borrowing a book."

"Talking with me? But you took out so many books."

He realized his direction had veered away from his purpose. "I like to read. That's not the point. The point is I've admired you and enjoyed your company from the beginning. I used the charade idea to spend time with you and get to know you better."

She stared at him, her eyes shifting from him to the distance and back as if she were trying to pull together threads of meaning from what he was saying.

"It's not a game anymore, Esther." He lifted his hand and caressed her cheek. "I really like you." He wanted to say more, but he hesitated, fearing he needed to study her reaction before dumping any more news on her. "And I enjoy being with you. So let's forget the charade and have fun together. You won't have guilt feelings over our friendship."

As if arising from a dream, Esther closed her eyes and opened them again, her face expressionless. "But when you kissed me at the Streetfest I asked why, and you said because Rachel and Jeff were watching us."

Ian lowered his gaze, feeling the pressure of his untruth. "No, that's not exactly what I said."

A deep frown wrinkled her brow. "But I'm sure—"

"I remember what happened. You asked why I'd kissed you. Then you asked, 'Were Rachel and Jeff watching us?' I answered 'Sure.'"

"Right, that's what you said."

"If you remember," he said, feeling guilty for his distortion of the truth, "they had been watching us, but not then. Not when I kissed you. But my answer was the truth."

Esther's distress softened. "But why didn't you tell me it was because you wanted to? That would have made all the difference."

All the difference? Now he was confused. "How?"

"Because I would have told you I wanted to be kissed."

Emotion kicked him in the ribs. He drew her closer, eye-to-eye, one hand on the wheel, and gazed into her eyes. "Are you telling me you feel the same? That you've wanted to be with me and..."

Before he finished his sentence, she nodded. "It didn't happen the day we met, but soon after." She rested her hand against his arm. "I really enjoy spending time with you, Ian. I—"

He silenced her words with a kiss. A small gasp escaped her lungs and her warm breath sent a shudder down his limbs.

His heart filled with pleasure as he felt her lips captured beneath his, and for the first time she yielded fully to his embrace, wrapping her arms around his neck. Her mouth tempted his in rhythm to their beating hearts.

The boat swayed, and Ian eased back and opened his eyes, gazing beyond Esther's countenance to study a passing sailboat. He glanced at the sky, noticing that the sun was lower than he'd expected. "I suppose we'd better head back." When he moved his foot, a telltale crunch sounded from the floor.

Esther shifted, and her laughter blended with the crackle beneath his feet. "Forget the chips," she said. "They're potato dust now."

Ian looked toward his feet to see the toppled sack, pulverized on the floor. He didn't care. Who cared about food when love filled him?

He shifted the crumbled chips aside with his feet, and his laughter joined hers, reminding him that he'd wanted to rename his sailboat. Maybe to commemorate this extraordinary day, he'd name the boat *Mr. Chips.*

Rachel twisted the engagement ring in circles on her finger as she stared at Jeff. "I want to wear it. You know I do, but I can't." She looked down at the lovely ring, the solitaire diamond flickering in the afternoon light. "I've already explained it to you."

"Let me get this straight." Refusing to sit, Jeff leaned against the door frame, his body tense, his words unyielding. "Your father sets up this hopeless situation based on the Bible. Then he tells you he's wrong, he's had second thoughts...but he won't change his mind."

With her voice knotting in her throat, Rachel only nodded.

"And you're going to follow along with this ridiculous line of thinking." Jeff laced the last words with sarcasm.

Trying to answer his double-bladed question, Rachel felt her words tangle in her heart. Tears rolled from her eyes and dripped onto her left hand. She brushed them away, and the diamond sent a spectrum of color into the air. A beautiful gem, but weighted with trouble. Rachel captured her courage. "Jeff, my father might be foolish and stubborn, but the Bible tells me to honor and obey him. I'm so confused. So frustrated. All I can ask you to do is give me a little more time. Let me—"

"Time!" His voice bounced off her apartment wall.

Rachel flinched at his anger.

"I've given you enough time to build a pyramid, Rachel. Look." He pulled his shoulder from the door frame and walked to her side, resting one hand on the chair back, the other on the upholstered arm. "I don't want to set up competition between your father and me. I'm happy if you love us both. But—"

"I do love you both," she said, pressing her hand against his. "I don't want to choose between you. I'm putting this in God's hands. Let God tell me what to do."

Jeff straightened, his back as rigid as a tin soldier. "Are you crazy? Have you lost your mind?"

Startled, she felt her heart hammer against her breastbone, and she lifted her hand to press against the thunder in her chest.

"When do you expect God will send you a letter?" He folded his arms across his chest. "Or will His voice break through the sky. 'Rachel Downing,'" Jeff boomed, his voice deepened, "'I am the Lord and you have My permission to wear Jeff's engagement ring.'" He cupped his hand around his ear, his face mottled. "I'm listening, Rachel, and I don't hear God saying a word."

Rachel clapped her hands over her ears to block his contempt. "Please don't do this, Jeff." She sat a moment, her heart crying out in prayer. Unexpected, a sense of calm washed over her along with a new realization. She rose and stepped toward Jeff, filled with purpose.

"Please listen." Her hand played with the ring as she riveted her gaze to his. "I can't ask you to understand my father...or my faith. I know you're a Christian, but apparently not one who feels the same connection to God's will as I do.''

Jeff's eyes shifted nervously, and his shoulders sagged as he returned his focus to her face. Rachel sensed he wanted to speak, but he didn't. He listened.

''I have to do what my faith directs me to do. I have to give this problem to God. I'm beginning to think that the Lord thinks we aren't meant for each other.''

''You what?'' He jammed his fist against the door frame. ''I don't get it.''

''We're different, Jeff. Our faith is different. I feel in my heart I love you, but I want our marriage to last. At this point, it can't.''

He stepped forward and captured her face in his hands, standing nose-to-nose. ''You're telling me you don't think we can make it? You know better, Rachel.''

Tears misted his eyes, and Rachel's chest tightened with a tourniquet of despair. She slipped the ring from her finger and clutched it in her hands.

He lowered his hands from her face, his own expression desperate and solemn. ''So...I'll wait. I can't lose you.''

She captured his hand and dropped the ring into his palm. ''I can't keep this now. Not unless things are settled.'' She prayed things would be better. That Jeff would back off and let God handle their problem.

Jeff's gaze dropped to the ring, and his mouth gaped. He drew up his shoulders and moved back, his eyes focused on his palm. "If you do this, Rachel, it's over. There's no coming back." He lifted his gaze to hers, searching her eyes as if hoping she would change her mind.

The words knocked her breath from her lungs. She studied him in disbelief. "You can't mean that."

"I do." His expression held defiance, but beneath it Rachel saw a glimmer of fear.

She let the weight of her decision settle in her thoughts. Rachel had no other choice. Only when she knew for certain—only when God gave her comfort and a solution—would she take back the ring...but Jeff had decreed their destiny. It had ended.

A shroud of silence hung over them as they stared at each other. Tentacles of pain moved through her, and her heart plunged as Jeff turned away and left the apartment.

Grinning, Ian watched Esther maneuver her way toward a booth at the Autumn Spice Craft Show. His spirit had soared since the day on the boat when he'd admitted his feelings. He'd wanted to confess he loved her, but he hadn't known what to expect from her. Her response had been much more than he'd hoped.

"Look at this silk arrangement," Esther said, lifting the basket of copper-colored flowers toward Ian. "Picture this on my end table."

Jostled by a shopper, Ian shifted to the side and eyed the bouquet. "I thought you were Christmas shopping."

She tilted her head and shrugged. "I'll gift wrap it and give it to myself."

Why didn't he discourage her and then come back to buy it? The ploy seemed too complicated. "Sure. Buy it. Everyone deserves at least one gift he buys himself at Christmas."

He'd done it himself. Bought something he longed to have as his own Christmas gift. Not living close to his family, Ian had often missed the excitement of decorating a tree and anticipating gifts. He sent packages to his sister's children. Sometimes he visited at the holidays, but always felt as if he were in the way. They had their own friends and activities, and he didn't want to add a third wheel to their holiday fun.

But this year would be different. A warm, cozy feeling settled in his chest. He and Esther would spend time together, and—if it weren't too soon— he'd thought he might propose at Christmas. The possibility shot anxious exhilaration to his toes.

"Maybe I'll wait," she said, returning the silk arrangement to the display and linking her arm in his. "I want to look at holiday wreaths. Something for Rachel's door. She doesn't have anything to hang there."

"Speaking of Rachel, how's she doing?" Ian asked, curious that Esther hadn't mentioned worrying about her lately. "Are things better between her and your dad?"

Esther slowed, then halted while passersby jostled around them. "Now that you mention it, I haven't spoken with her in over a week. That's strange."

He eyed her face, seeing it fill with concern, and

Ian hoped nothing had happened. Esther's guilt over the charade had set her on edge, and he didn't want to deal with any more repercussions. "Maybe she's just busy."

"Maybe," Esther said, "but she usually calls anyway. She talked with Dad and said she wouldn't be in church last Sunday." A frown settled on her face. "I should have called her to find out why."

"You can telephone her when you get home."

She nodded. "Right. Remind me, would you?"

"I'll try," he said, knowing in his heart he didn't want to remind her. An uneasy feeling dampened his spirit. If something unpleasant had happened between Rachel and Jeff, Esther would be in the doldrums. When Esther felt stressed, Ian seemed to feel tense himself, and tonight they'd been invited for dinner at the Somervilles'. He'd hoped it would be an enjoyable evening.

Ian glanced at his wristwatch. "What time do you think we'll get out of here?" He'd never seen such a huge craft show. It filled every hallway and room of the St. Patrick Center, and they'd been there at least an hour already.

"I don't know. Why?"

"I want to change before we go to Philip's tonight," he said.

Her expression changed as she was jolted with a thought. "A hostess gift. That's what I need. Help me think of something for them."

"Esther, they aren't expecting a gift. I'll pick up a bouquet at the florist, if you'd like."

Searching the displays they passed, she shook her

head. "No. I want this to be special…and something from me."

He grinned. "Feeling guilty?"

She expelled a soft chuckle. "Maybe a little. You should have heard the things I imagined about Jemma when I thought that was you and her in the photograph."

"Don't tell me. I have my own memories to deal with."

"I suppose you do," she said, releasing his arm and sliding her hand into his with a gentle squeeze.

The closeness of them walking together side by side, their hands joined, had become a gift for which Ian felt grateful. He thanked God often for giving him the courage to admit his feelings and for Esther's accepting reaction to his confession. He squeezed her hand in return, relishing the tenderness between them.

At one booth after another, Esther stopped to eye the items and to weigh her decisions. If Ian had had his way, he'd have sat in the snack section and waited, but Esther insisted he follow along to offer his opinion. He settled into the role, sensing this would be part of his relationship with Esther. Sharing everything.

"Burgundy and gold," she said, holding a door wreath in front of her with one finger. "I love the colors."

"Nice," he said. He'd said that about four others, and he hoped she wouldn't notice.

"I think Rachel will like it," Esther said, handing

the gift to the woman behind the table, then digging into her wallet.

"Me, too," Ian said, relieved that particular purchase had been settled.

With the wreath in a large shopping bag, Esther led him toward a stained glass booth. A backlit screen displayed a variety of sun catchers. Her attention seemed drawn to a beveled glass cross. The bright blue sparkled in the light.

"For Dad," she said. "He loves looking out his windows, and I think this cross is perfect."

Without asking his opinion, she paid for the gift, and they moved along until she found the perfect hostess gift. After some time, Ian got antsy and reminded Esther of their dinner plans.

Surprised, she suggested they leave, and when they arrived at her house, she climbed out loaded down with packages in both arms.

"Need help?" he asked.

"No. You go ahead. I'll see you in an hour."

He gave her a wave and backed down the driveway. As he did, he remembered he was supposed to remind her to call Rachel. Though he could have gone back, he guided the car to the street, feeling guilty but hopeful that she'd forgotten and he wouldn't have to deal with any Rachel issues tonight.

Esther stood near the window waiting for Ian to return. She'd just finished dressing and knew he would arrive any minute. She could count on his being on time.

The past few days she'd enjoyed spending time

with him. Since they'd talked in earnest about their feelings, she no longer wondered how he felt about her. He'd admitted he enjoyed her company just as she enjoyed his.

They'd declared a real friendship, and he'd kissed her. The kiss seemed to signal more than a friendly relationship. She'd enjoyed every minute of his intimate caress, but did it constitute something more serious? She wasn't so sure about that.

Years ago she'd declared herself a single woman for a lifetime, but now her behavior suggested something different—a new yearning for companionship. She'd prayed to the Lord to give her confidence in herself and in His bidding.

When she thought about it, her heart reacted as if it were love, and Esther longed to make their relationship a lasting one. But her thoughts and feelings left her feeling vulnerable, and Esther feared that if Ian didn't feel as strongly, she had opened herself for hurt and grief.

Lights flashed across the driveway, and Ian pulled in. Without waiting, Esther grabbed the hostess gift, locked the house and hurried to the car.

During the short ride they talked about the resort and Philip mainly, but Esther's mind had stuck on a question. Was her relationship with Ian heading anywhere?

At Bay Breeze she and Ian stepped into the elevator and rode up to the penthouse. Carrying the gift bag, Esther stepped across the threshold and faced Jemma.

Seeing the woman closely, Esther could understand Ian's earlier attraction to her. Jemma extended her slender arm beyond her protruding belly where Philip's first child lay, warm and safe, and offered them her hand.

"It's good to see you, Jemma," Ian said. "This is Esther Downing."

"I'm glad to meet you," Esther said with a firm handshake.

Jemma's generous mouth curved to a gentle smile, and she looked at Esther with green eyes the color of moss. "Welcome. I'm so glad you could come."

"Thank you," Esther said, feeling Ian's hand on her arm, guiding her forward. "This is such a lovely place. I was here for the Fourth of July celebration."

Jemma wagged her head. "So many people. I can never do them all justice."

"It was a wonderful party," Esther said, extending the gift bag. "Here's a little something for you."

Jemma lifted her hand to her chest. "For us? Oh, you shouldn't have." With an appreciative look, she accepted the gift. "Thank you."

"Ian and I were at the Autumn Spice Craft Show today and I thought you'd like it."

"I'm sure we will. Have a seat. Please," Jemma said, motioning them into the great room and setting the package on an end table.

Tonight the French doors were closed against a cool northern breeze, but Esther recalled the wonderful view of the lake. She crossed to a love seat and Ian followed.

Jemma gave them an apologetic smile. "Philip is

in the kitchen, concocting a fruit punch. I'll send him out.''

''Punch sounds good,'' Ian said.

Jemma's soft-soled shoes padded across the floor. When she vanished, Ian slid his arm around Esther. ''What are you thinking?'' he asked.

''I can see why you found her attractive.''

''Jealous?'' He stroked her cheek with his free hand.

''Should I be?''

His chuckle said no, but before he could speak, Philip strode into the room with a tray of stemmed glasses. ''Greetings. I was whipping up drinks.''

''We heard,'' Ian said.

Philip extended the tray, and Esther took a fluted glass. The fruity aroma drifted from the tray.

Behind Philip, Jemma hurried in and set a platter of hors d'oeuvres and cocktail napkins on the nearby coffee table. ''Help yourself,'' she said. ''Dinner will be ready shortly.''

Philip leaned forward. ''By the way, Esther, I've studied your report. Found it fascinating and very creative. It's been very helpful in my decision making for next year. In fact, let's drink a toast.'' Philip lifted his glass. ''To the future.''

''To your new baby,'' Esther added.

Jemma gave her an appreciative smile before sipping the punch.

Esther lifted her glass and took a drink of the unique fruit juice blend. The creamy taste of coconut created a tantalizing flavor with the citrus mixture. ''Delicious.''

"Philip doesn't want people to know he reads cookbooks as a hobby."

Their chuckles were sprinkled around the room, and as Jemma turned to find a seat, she spotted the gift. "Look, Philip," she said, lifting the bag from the table. "Esther's brought us a present."

"A gift? That was thoughtful," he said. "Should we open it?"

"Yes. Please," Esther said.

They waited as Jemma pulled the tissue from the bag and unwrapped a small watercolor. She released a surprised gasp as she turned the painting to Philip. "It's beautiful, and so fitting here."

Philip eyed the scene—a sailboat with a wash of sunset on the horizon. "We have a perfect spot for it." He rose and placed the painting against the wall near the French doors. "It's a small area, and we've had nothing to hang here."

"It looks lovely," Jemma said. "Thank you so much." She bent and kissed Esther's cheek.

"You're welcome," Esther said, pleased that her hosts liked the painting.

Jemma turned toward the coffee table and picked up napkins and the platter. "Let me get you started on these," she said, handing Esther a napkin and explaining the choices.

"I'm so glad Ian brought you along. Philip mentioned you two were working on a research project together, and it made me chuckle."

Esther felt Ian stiffen beside her as she selected appetizers.

"I don't know if Ian told you," she continued.

"Philip had us running here and there a while back, working on a project together."

Esther gave a slight nod, fearing what she might say next.

"My dearest Philip—" she gave him a smile as she replaced the napkins and platter onto the table "—wanted me to find a husband. I think Ian was his first choice."

Ian squirmed beside her. "I don't know about—"

"She's right, Ian. I thought I was too old for Jemma. You were perfect—a good employee, a man I trusted, one I thought would be a good husband and a gentleman."

"Thanks, Philip, but—"

"And look at us now," Jemma said, patting her tummy.

"Congratulations," Esther said, hoping to veer the topic to children and families and away from Ian.

"Philip thought he was too old to be a father, but God and I thought different."

Her comment captured Esther's attention. She understood. Esther had made a life decision, giving credit to God, and now she wondered if her decision to be single had been her own distorted thinking— her own self-defense.

"So often—just like Philip did—we decide things about ourselves. After Philip's first wife died, he'd determined marriage was out of the question." She moved beside him and ran her hand across his shoulder. "I'd thought the same for myself. One bad marriage was enough for me, but God had different ideas."

"That's exactly the way it happened," Philip said, raising his hand and placing it on hers, which rested on his shoulder. "Here I was pushing her toward Ian and God was pushing me toward Jemma."

To Esther's surprise, Ian began to chuckle. She felt his rigid body relax beside her, and the room quieted, everyone waiting for him to explain.

"Thanks for getting all this out in the open, Jemma. Every time I see you, my mind sails back to that whole situation. Even though I wasn't sure whether our relationship would ever go anywhere, I still felt rejected when you dumped me for Philip."

His smile assured Esther he meant what he said.

"I know," Jemma said. "And I felt guilty about the whole situation. I loved Philip from the start and felt rejected by him, pushing me away."

Philip wagged his hand across the air like an erasure. "It's all over now. God's worked out everything. Jemma and I. Ian and Esther."

The reference to them as a couple sent a rush of heat up her neck. "My sister and Jeff," Esther added, to draw attention away from her and Ian.

"Yes. I forgot about that," Jemma said. "That's so nice. They are a darling couple. I've seen them often at the resort events."

Philip shifted in his chair while his expression changed to a frown.

"What's wrong?" Jemma asked.

"Mentioning Jeff made me think," he said. "I've been meaning to talk to him. Jeff's missed a couple of days recently and it just doesn't seem right. Something's wrong."

Something's wrong. The words jolted Esther and frustration shuffled up her back as she remembered she'd forgotten to call Rachel. She saw Ian give her a quick look, then turn back toward the others.

But the rest of the discourse was lost on Esther. Something was wrong. Something had happened between Jeff and Rachel. Esther sensed it, and she wanted to know what had happened.

Chapter Fifteen

Esther closed her eyes and pressed her fingers against her temples. She sensed Rachel had been avoiding her. She'd called throughout the week, over and over, and now on Friday night Esther still knew nothing. *It's in God's hands* was all Rachel would say.

Why couldn't Rachel's philosophy be her own expression of faith? Putting her troubles in God's hands. Esther rubbed her eyes again, then massaged the back of her tension-knotted neck. How could she enjoy an evening with Ian when her sister occupied her mind?

The scent of the chicken cooking in the oven filled the air, but her stomach churned without appetite. The past days, she'd wanted to enjoy Ian's company, but her sister's withdrawal had filled Esther with resentment. Resentment for the charade and everything she and Ian had done to cause Rachel grief. If they'd stayed out of it, Rachel and Jeff might still have had problems, but Esther knew she'd be innocent of any meddling. Tonight guilt sat on her like an elephant.

When a tap sounded from outside, Esther rose and opened the door, letting in a brisk scent of autumn. Ian stood on the porch, his suede jacket zipped to the neck.

"Hi," he said, a puff of white vapor emerging with his word.

"It's cold out there." A shiver ran down Esther's back.

He puffed another cloud of warm-against-cold air. "You can say that again. I think the temperature dropped twenty degrees in the past hour." He shifted his feet. "Can I come in?"

"Sure," she said, embarrassed at her distraction. She pushed open the door. "I don't know where my mind is." She knew, but she didn't want to talk about it now.

Though Ian always noticed her mood, most of the time he kept the knowledge to himself. She could often see his mind churning with questions, but he'd apparently learned that riling her with questions only caused more distress for both of them.

In the foyer Ian slipped off his jacket and hooked it on the coatrack. "Something smells great," he said, striding into the living room.

"Stewed chicken with potatoes and carrots."

"And dumplings?"

A faint grin tugged at her mouth while she nodded. "Would you like a drink?"

He grasped her hand and beckoned her toward him. "I'd like you better."

"Me?"

He tilted her chin and brushed a kiss along her lips.

"You're freezing," she said, feeling the cold from outdoors on his clothing, using the distraction to cover her reaction to his kiss.

"I know, but I need warming up." He wrapped his icy hands around her back, sending a chill down her spine, and held her close, nestling his frigid cheek against hers.

"Yikes," she yowled. "You're an ice cube."

Chuckling, he pulled away and headed for a chair.

"Dinner's nearly ready if you want to come to the table," she said, gesturing toward the dining room.

He eyed her, sensing her distraction, she was sure. He didn't ask what was wrong, but followed her suggestion as she headed for the kitchen.

In a few moments Esther carried the food to the table, and after the blessing Ian filled his plate while she selected a small piece of meat and a couple of vegetables.

Though he appeared to enjoy the meal, Ian ate in near silence with only an occasional compliment to her about the meal. Observing his behavior, she knew he longed to ask what was wrong, but he didn't.

In the restrained silence Esther's stomach twisted with each bite, and in frustration she pushed back her plate.

Ian noted her action and lowered his fork. "I've avoided asking...but what's up?"

She shrugged. "I don't know."

"Don't be evasive, Esther. Is it Rachel?"

She nodded. "She won't talk and I'm frustrated and concerned. I left another message on her machine an hour ago and left her a Bible quote. I hope that motivates her to talk."

He grasped his fork again. "I hope so." He took a bite, swallowed, then looked at her again. "What are you thinking?"

"I'm feeling guilty." The spoken words made the reality even worse. "I'm sure Rachel and Jeff are having problems. They've probably had a terrible argument, and you and I have resolved ours. Why should I be happy now that Rachel's life is a mess?"

"But you didn't cause the mess." He reached across the table and grasped her hand. "And our relationship has nothing to do with Rachel's."

"But it does. Don't you get it?"

"I guess not. You'll have to explain—"

Before he finished his sentence, the telephone rang. Esther's heart leaped to her throat, and she pushed away her frustration with Ian. She tugged her hand from his, shoved her chair away from the table and rose. "I hope this is Rachel."

Leaving Ian alone in the dining room, she hurried to the kitchen and grabbed the phone. Rachel's strident voice struck her ear.

"Will you talk with me?" Esther pleaded. "Tell me what's happened."

"I wish you'd let me be," Rachel said.

"Well, I won't. This is about you and Jeff, isn't it?"

A long silence lingered until she responded, "Yes, it's over."

"Over? What do you mean, it's over?" Her heart tripped in her chest, sending her pulse skyrocketing. She'd hoped it had only been an argument. A simple, solvable disagreement.

"Just what I said." Tears sounded in her voice.

"What can I do to help you, Rachel? Please. We need to talk."

Another hush fell on the wire.

"Not on the phone," Rachel said finally.

"I'll come over, then." She pictured Ian waiting at her table, but it didn't matter. He had caused the problem more than she had. He needed to understand what he'd done. "I'll come over now. Okay?"

"It's up to you," Rachel whispered.

Esther hung up and drew in a calming breath. What could she say to Ian? Words tumbled through her head. Words and accusations. She needed to control her frustration. Control her anger at herself and Ian for allowing the charade to happen.

She clung to the doorjamb until she'd steadied herself, then headed through the archway into the dining room. "I have to go. I'm sorry."

Ian shot from his chair. "What's wrong?"

"That was Rachel." Sorrow caught in her throat. "She and Jeff have...broken off their engagement." She compressed the bridge of her nose. "I knew it. I just knew it."

"I'm sorry," he said, slipping his arm around her shoulders.

Without control, she jerked away from his touch. "Don't, Ian."

He recoiled. "What did I do?"

"I feel guilty enough. Rachel has no one because of your foolish idea."

He teetered backward. "We've talked about this before, Esther. I'm willing to take the blame for the idea, but I'm not willing to be punished for Rachel's problems. They're between her and Jeff, not—"

"If you hadn't suggested the charade, Rachel wouldn't have had unrealistic hopes. Maybe she and Jeff could have dealt with things on their own. By believing we were serious about each other, they expected everything to fall into place. They let down their guard and made plans. Plans that failed."

"Esther—"

"Don't deny it. Their making plans and getting their hopes up is your fault. It was that stupid idea."

He stepped toward her, but she raised her hands to fend him off. "No. I'm not going to be happy when I caused my sister so much pain. Think about it, Ian. Think about how this all began."

She spun away and tugged her coat from the foyer closet. "I'm leaving."

Ian passed her and grabbed his coat from the hook, then tugged open the door. A gust of wind sailed through the foyer and vanished when Ian slammed it shut. Esther stared at the closed door.

Ian had gone.

Heading away from Esther's, Ian swallowed the emotion that ambushed his throat. Why had he let this happen? What could he have done to avoid the horrible confrontation? He tried to understand. He knew one thing for sure—he shouldn't have walked out on Esther. That had been a mistake.

Never let the sun go down on your wrath. He could hear his mother's voice. Was that Scripture or just an old saying? He wasn't sure, but the words were as true as a new day.

Wrestling with what to do now, Ian thought of Jeff. If he talked with him, maybe he'd understand what had happened and what had upset Esther so badly.

He eyed his car clock. Eight on a Friday night. Sometimes Jeff worked evenings at the resort. Ian turned at the next signal light and headed for Bay Breeze, hoping to find Jeff there. He needed to know what had happened between him and Rachel, but as much, he needed to collect himself.

When he pulled into the parking lot, Ian turned off the motor and sat, wishing he could erase the past hour and start it over again. Why hadn't he reasoned with Esther? Why hadn't he overlooked what she'd said? The answer was clear. Because he'd felt rejected again. The same old problem.

Esther had been upset, and her words were evidence of her frustration and anger at herself as well as him. Instead of letting it blow over, he'd stormed out like a fool. The blunder stuck in his mind.

Trying to decide what to do about Esther, he weighed his options. He could let a couple of hours pass and call her. Or maybe he'd be wise to wait until tomorrow. With a day to soften their angry words, the disagreement could be resolved in minutes. Tomorrow he might even show up at her door.

Ian pulled his keys from the ignition and opened the car door. A gust of wind pressed against it, making him strain to get outside. Thinking of the weather, he knew he'd have to get the boat stored soon. He'd waited longer than usual. Optimistic, he always hoped Indian summer would honor autumn and give him a few more days of sailing weather before the long winter lull. Images of his last sail with Esther filled his mind along with sadness. She might never know the surprise he'd planned for her.

Tugging his jacket around him, Ian strode across the parking lot and into the building. He followed the corridor to the lobby and felt relief when he spotted Jeff behind the registration desk.

Jeff lifted his hand in greeting.

Ian nodded and headed his way. "Do you have a minute?" he asked, approaching the counter.

Jeff's face tensed, and his brow wrinkled with inquiry. "You mean—"

"Privately," Ian added.

His unsettled expression turned to puzzlement, and Jeff turned to his co-worker. "Leslie, can you handle things for a few minutes?"

The woman nodded, and Jeff gave Ian a fleeting glance before he vanished through the doorway.

Ian met him in the hall. "Esther is in a fury, and she's on her way to see Rachel. Can you tell me what's happened?"

Jeff's face convulsed with emotion. "You mean Rachel hasn't said anything until now?" As if unbelieving, he shook his head. "That's all I think about, and she hasn't said a word to Esther."

"Well, she has by now. Esther has been trying to talk with her, and finally in the middle of dinner Rachel called. When she got off the phone, Esther attacked me for what's happened and—"

"You?"

"Pretending we were serious. But I was serious. It wasn't a game to me. I just let Esther think so."

Jeff looked confused.

"Anyway, I stormed out of the house, and now I don't know what to do. I thought if I knew what happened between you and Rachel, I'd have a clue what I'm up against."

"She broke our engagement. Handed me back the ring."

Ian listened as Jeff told him the details—her father's stubbornness, Jeff's demand to elope, Rachel's decision to put it in God's hands.

While Jeff's words sailed through his head, Ian's mind cleared. He and Esther could go nowhere until they both realized what Rachel had learned. God is in charge. God's will be done.

He saw what had happened to her father's manipulation. It had failed. So had Jeff and Rachel's attempt to interest Esther in someone they had chosen for her. Only when God's blessing touched a purpose could anyone be assured of success. Ian knew what he had to do.

"I love you," Rachel said, her arms around Esther's shoulders. "Thanks for coming over. I feel better."

"A little more hopeful, I'd like to hear."

Rachel shrugged. "I don't want to get too confident. I really want to be open to God's will." She dropped her arm, a look of sadness covering her face. "I'm beginning to think God knows my relationship with Jeff won't last."

"Why don't you think it would?" Esther asked, her mind filled with disbelief.

"It's not what I think, but maybe it's a sign from God." She lowered her head, her mouth twitching with emotion.

"Don't put words in God's mouth, Rachel. Let time be the judge of what will happen. You and Jeff both spouted off. You were upset and angry...but remember, the anger was more at Dad and my involvement in this mess than at each other."

Rachel gave a faint nod.

"No matter, talking with Dad is necessary. Even if you and Jeff don't get back together, we need to get this solved for the future." Esther picked up her purse. "I'm not going to spend my life fighting off everyone's attempts to marry me off to some poor unsuspecting single guy, like you and Jeff were doing."

Rachel gave her a faint grin. "I am so sorry about that. I shouldn't have listened to Jeff."

The same thought spiraled through Esther. She shouldn't have listened to Ian. Esther clasped the doorknob. "Anyway, we've agreed to forgive and... try to forget all of this, and I'll give you a call so we can talk about how we'll handle all this with Dad."

Rachel nodded. "We need to sleep on it."

"And say lots of prayers."

Rachel leaned over and kissed Esther's cheek. "Thanks again, Esther."

"Will you sleep?"

"I hope so," she said.

Esther made her exit and headed home, her nerves constricted, her mind tired. They'd talked and it had been good. A talk that had brought them together. A talk that had healed. During their difficult dialogue, they'd asked for and offered each other forgiveness. She hadn't felt this close to Rachel in years.

Glancing at the dashboard, she noticed the time. Eleven. She remembered the dinner still sitting on the dining-room table. Food she'd have to toss in the trash. Then her thought shifted to Ian. Ian whose anger had shocked her.

She'd been right, she'd thought at the time. Now…she wasn't sure. She couldn't even remember what she'd said to him. Tomorrow she'd sort it out and see what it all meant.

Maybe Rachel was right. Maybe this was God's way of validating her earlier belief. Esther Downing was meant to be single.

Turning down her street, Esther could think of nothing but clean sheets and a soft pillow. As she approached her house, her headlights flashed against a bumper and red reflectors on a car parked in front. Some neighbor had company, she assumed.

Esther pulled into the driveway and located her house key on the ring. As she slid the key into the lock, a shadow blocked the streetlight and her heart lurched.

"Can we talk?"

Ian's voice sounded behind her, and she turned with a mixture of relief and disbelief. "It's late."

"I know it's late. I've been waiting out here for nearly two hours."

She looked at him in the lamplight. "I'm tired, Ian."

"I'm tired, too, but I think this is important."

Esther's heart sank as she wondered what to do. She'd already said so many things she wished she hadn't. Yet part of her knew they had to be said. She needed time to think and sort through her feelings.

"You won't wait until tomorrow?"

His look gave her his answer. She turned the key in the lock and pushed open the door. They walked through the kitchen, and out of habit she almost offered him coffee or tea, but this wasn't the time or situation for amenities.

She sank into a chair and looked at him.

Instead of sitting, he stood by the door, his hands jammed in his coat pockets. "I'm sorry I stormed out of here earlier."

"It was my fault. I pushed you out the door, but Rachel needed me. She's my only sister and—"

He took a step forward. "I'd probably drop everything and rush to my sister if I thought she needed me. I understand."

Silence hovered over them like a shroud.

Esther glanced at her wristwatch.

"I know I'm keeping you, but I'd hoped that we could...I don't know..." He wanted to say kiss and make up, but the lighthearted line would anger her.

Tonight she was more sensitive than he'd ever seen her.

"Could what? We apologized to each other. That's progress."

Her words sounded distant and uncaring. "It's a small step," he said.

"I can't give you more than that tonight. I'm confused and tired. I need time to think about my life and figure out what I want in it." She rose. "I've enjoyed your company. We had business to do, and being amiable about it made it easier."

"Amiable? Wasn't it a little more than amiable?" His hair prickled at the nape of his neck. Coming tonight had been a mistake. Ian could see they were getting nowhere…except perhaps digging the hole deeper.

"I don't know what I think." She turned her back and looked away from him. "Maybe this is God validating my decision years ago. I should never have gotten so close to you, Ian." She spun around to face him. "I let you go against my beliefs."

"You did what?" He heard his voice rise in pitch and volume. Anger had never been his friend. He didn't know how to handle it, and he'd rarely experienced it with a woman. Maybe because he'd never loved a woman before.

"I didn't want to play that game. It went against everything I stand for. Honesty. Faithfulness to family. Confidence. I doubted myself and let you cause me to fall."

"Look. I apologized for my part in this thing, but I'm not going to grovel to make you see the truth."

He stepped back, unable to believe what had happened. "The charade was a joint venture. My idea. Your participation. I'll sit in judgment for my part...but not for yours. Think about it, Esther."

Shocked at his own emotion, Ian felt tears rim his eyes. Why had this happened? He gave her one last look before opening the door. "No matter what you think, you've meant more to me than anything in the world."

He opened the door and stepped outside, trembling and depressed. He'd been so sure about his feelings for Esther. But now he needed time to think. Unless Esther loved him beyond all earthly troubles and concerns—for better or worse—a relationship would be impossible.

Rachel entered his mind. He needed to do what she'd done. Turn his problem over to God.

As he stepped from the porch, a cool breeze ruffled his collar, and he hurried to the car, forcing himself not to look back.

Chapter Sixteen

Esther sat at a red signal light, her thoughts writhing between her own problems and Rachel's. The past week they'd talked daily and had dinner together two evenings. Both felt lonely and burdened with sadness. Though Jeff had called Rachel asking to see her, Rachel had only repeated her litany. *It's in God's hands.*

But Esther? She'd stared at the telephone and jumped with each ring, only to hear Rachel or a telemarketer. Ian had not called since she'd sent him away.

Esther turned right, heading for Rachel's apartment, the problems weighing heavily on her thoughts. Today she and Rachel would talk with their father. They'd plotted their course and prayed to God to give them a gentle breeze and a calm sea.

Her thoughts washed over her in nostalgia as images of Ian at the helm of *Lady Day* rose before her. He'd never renamed the boat as he'd wanted, and the recollection deepened her yearning. They'd spent lovely moments on the sailboat, and she was grateful for the new, brighter sailing memories...though now touched by a different kind of sadness. She missed Ian.

Pulling into the lot, Esther parked and headed for the apartment building. The past days had been a heavenly gift. Indian summer. Gorgeous balmy, sun-filled days enveloped in burnished leaves.

She wondered if Ian had put the boat into storage or if he were enjoying the sunshine with a last sail or two before the cold days of winter.

Before Esther reached the outside door, Rachel appeared from the building and waved. Esther paused, waiting for her.

"Nervous?" Esther asked.

"A little. I hope Dad's in a good mood."

Esther put her hand on her sister's shoulder and gave it a squeeze. "I prayed a lot about this."

"Me, too," Rachel said, a chuckle mixed with her words.

"Then let's be positive."

Esther returned to the car, and Rachel slid into the passenger seat.

"Jeff just called again," Rachel said.

"What did he say this time?" Esther kept her eyes on her driving and pulled out from the parking lot.

Rachel shifted beneath her seat belt and faced Esther more directly. "He sounds different," Rachel said. "Quieter and...more serious."

Esther glanced toward her sister. "And what does that mean?"

"I don't know, except he's asked me to forgive him and tells me he loves me."

A sigh escaped Esther, imagining Jeff's motives. "He has to *be* serious...not just sound serious. I guess that's my only worry."

"I think he is. I really think so...but then I wonder if he'll just go back to being the same pushy man. I'm so confused, Esther."

"Pray about it. That's all you can do, and hopefully God will put the answer in your heart."

Rachel nodded and shifted straighter in her seat. "He sent me flowers," she murmured, as if it was a private afterthought.

Flowers? Esther had never received flowers from a man. A hush fell over the car while Esther pondered what she'd say to her father. She'd prayed often since she and Rachel had decided to confront him. She'd asked for God's blessing on the impending discussion and for the right words. She'd put it in God's hands.

The house came into view, and Esther pulled into the driveway, her pulse increasing as the car slowed. Her father's face appeared between the dining-room curtains. Seeing him, she sent another quick prayer to heaven.

As they reached the porch, the door opened and her father's smile greeted them. "Now, now. Both my girls at one time. This is an honor." He pushed back the storm door, and Esther held it for Rachel to enter first.

The word *honor* struck her like the backlash of a punching bag. She had to do this and still honor her father. *Lord, grant me the right words.* Her silent prayer soared to heaven as she closed the door behind her.

She kissed her dad's cheek and steered him into the living room. Rachel stood in the middle of the floor, tears already brimming in her eyes.

"What's wrong?" her father asked.

"We have to talk," Esther said. "Let's sit."

Her father's face flooded with mottled fear. He grasped the chair arms and sank into the cushion, his eyes shifting from her to Rachel and back.

"Someone die?" he asked.

"No. Only Rachel's and my spirits. It's your stubborn insistence, Dad." She let the words flow from her mind to her throat. "Rachel and I love and honor you, but we're hearing a different message from God than you are."

"I don't know what you mean," her father said.

"We need to share ideas about this marriage thing, Dad, and find the truth and our heavenly Father's will in this mess."

Though his back had stiffened a moment, he sank against the chair with her last words.

Rachel pulled out a Bible from her large shoulder bag. "I've been reading the Scriptures over and over, Dad." She flipped open to a page she'd marked with a yellow sticky note. "See, right here." She pointed. "The Lord says people need partners. Mates to pick them up when they fall or defend them when an enemy tries to hurt them."

"We all need friends," her father said.

"There's more. Read this. Chapter four, verse eleven in Ecclesiastes." She handed him the Bible.

Her father took it from her and squinted at the words.

"Read it out loud," Rachel said.

He gave her a scowl before doing as she asked. "'Also, if two lie down together, they will keep warm. But how can one keep warm alone?'" He peered at her. "What do you want me to say?"

"Say that's not a description of friendship," she said, her voice reflecting her irritation. "Friends don't sleep together. That's God's description of marriage."

Rachel took the Bible from his hands. "I have more verses, Dad. You know them by heart. A man will leave his father and mother's home and be united to his wife as one flesh. This Scripture has no regulations about who's older than who."

Watching her father's face, Esther stepped in. "Dad, you've already admitted that you were wrong saying your viewpoint was the Bible's instruction."

She crossed the room, knelt beside him and rested her forehead on his hand clamped to the chair arm. "Two people love each other and want to marry. God's will is what counts." She lifted her gaze to his, praying for God to be with her. "We can't manipulate that. If God has led Rachel to the man she should marry before I've made that decision, you're foiling God's will by demanding she wait."

Rachel burst into tears. "It doesn't even matter anymore, Dad. Jeff and I aren't seeing each other."

Her father's head bolted upward. "No. You don't mean that."

"She does," Esther said. "I'm not seeing Ian, either."

Disappointment flooded his face. "But...he was a good man, Esther. You looked happy together." He shifted his gaze to Rachel. "I'd longed to see you girls happy with a worthy man. Your mother and I shared so many wonderful years...and I miss her so much."

A mist of tears pooled in his eyes. "I'd only hoped to see both of you married and happy. I wanted your mother to enjoy some grandchildren...but God had other plans there." He took a swipe at his eyes with the back of his hand. "I thought that if Rachel married...Esther would never come out of her shell...."

"We know what you thought, Dad," Esther said, "but it's not fair to Rachel or to me."

"It's not," he said, his head drooping, his eyes focused at the floor. "I'm sorry. I pray God forgives me and you—"

"God forgives us, Daddy," Rachel said, slipping an arm around her father's shoulders. "And we forgive you, too. We just want you to let us live our lives."

"Your mother's probably up in heaven shaking her fist at me...and all I wanted was to see both of you as content as your mother and I were."

"We will be, Dad," Esther said. "In our own way."

He looked at them with sorrowful eyes. "No hope to patch things up for either of you?"

"It's in God's hands, Daddy," Rachel said. "So far, the Lord's handling things better than I ever did alone, so you never know."

Esther didn't comment. Her hopes had faded, and at this moment she didn't see any shining possibilities. She'd thought Ian would call her the day after their argument, but he hadn't, and the more she reviewed the angry words she'd flung at him, the more she wondered if she even deserved a man as good as Ian. Questions without answers marched through her head. She needed to think…and pray.

Her dad tilted his head upward, shifting his gaze from one to the other. "Would you girls go to church with me tomorrow?"

"Sure, Daddy," Rachel said. "That'll be nice." But her voice was soft, and Esther knew her mind was still tangled with Jeff and their situation.

Without hesitation, Esther nodded, knowing church was where she needed to be. She also realized she and Rachel had more things to settle before they left their father's house.

Rachel opened the door, her pulse pounding as she looked at Jeff.

"Thanks for letting me come over," he said, his hand clutching the storm door frame.

Rachel stepped back, longing to throw her arms around his neck, yearning to kiss his sad face. Though she'd agreed to his visit, she'd promised herself not to say a word about the talk with her father. She needed to know Jeff loved her and would stick by her in times of trial as well as happiness. Would he pick her up when she fell? Protect her against an enemy? Keep her warm, even when she angered him? Stifled by confusion, Rachel felt her words jam against her throat.

Instead, she gestured, and Jeff stepped toward a chair. When he sat, she studied him a moment, his reddish-blond hair windblown and his gaze shy and uncertain. Her heart stirred at the look of loneliness in his eyes.

"Thanks for the flowers," she said finally. "They're beautiful."

"Not as beautiful as…" His words died away.

She knew he wanted to say *as beautiful as you,* but he didn't, and she understood. This wasn't time for flattery, but time for truth.

"You wanted to talk," she said.

Leaning with his elbows against his knees, his eyes focused on his feet, he said, "I've done a lot of thinking, Rachel." He lifted his head slightly, enough for his gaze to meet hers. "And I've been praying."

Praying? He rarely talked about prayer. Was this one of his coy attempts to make her think he'd changed? She gave him a questioning look.

"I've given a lot of thought to what you said, and you're right," he said.

Her skin prickled with his admission, but uncertainty still pushed away her desire to trust him. "I'm right?"

"You know I'm not much of a Bible reader. I listen to the verses in church. I didn't grow up with a family who took much stock in religion, but I did read the Bible later…on my own. Even more since I met you.''

She didn't know where he was headed, but she listened.

''Anyway…I'm not saying what I mean.'' He dragged in a breath and released it. ''I'm nervous.''

''Why?''

''Because I love you so much and I'm losing you.''

His plaintive statement rippled through her chest and settled in her heart. ''Jeff, you know I've loved you. You're the only man I've been with…forever, it seems, but we're looking at life differently. I can't—''

''Let me finish,'' he said, dangling his clasped hands between his knees and leaning forward as if trying to be as near as his distance would allow. ''Being away from you these past days has helped me weigh what's important in life. And what's important is you. Life is nothing without you. It's an empty void.''

Looking at the pleading in his face, Rachel caught her breath.

''My understanding of the Bible isn't as strong as yours, but my faith is. I trust that God makes all things happen for good. In my heart, I think we're good…together.'' Jeff rose and knelt at Rachel's side. ''If I can't have you now as a wife, then I want you to be my best friend. And the woman I'll marry when the time is right.''

The meaning sank into her thoughts, gentle and

weightless like a feather on the wind. "Are you saying you'll wait?"

He grasped her hands. "If necessary, I'll wait forever. Being with you is a thousand times better than being without you. Marriage will happen in God's time. I believe that with every bone in my body."

Rachel struggled to control her emotions. Tears bubbled behind her eyes and surged forward to be freed.

"Please forgive me for my impatience. I love you and always will."

Her tears won the battle, streaming from her eyes and dripping to his hands clasping hers. "I forgive you, Jeff. I hope you forgive me for not being more understanding."

He rose and drew her from the chair into his embrace. "Love forgives everything," he whispered.

His lips lowered to hers and she clung to him, feeling secure and content for the first time since he'd been gone. She eased back, gazing into his concerned eyes. "I love you. Heart and soul."

She felt him fumble in his shirt pocket, and she inched back to see what he was doing. Catching a glint of flashing color, she knew he'd brought back the engagement ring in hope that she'd accept it.

"Will you take back the ring? Keep it somewhere until you can wear it? I promise not to bug you about it."

She lifted her hand and extended it toward him. "Would you put it on my finger?"

With uncertainty he studied her face, then did as she asked.

The ring glinted fire in the lamplight, but her love burned with greater intensity. "I'll never take it off."

A puzzled look grew on his face. "But—"

"Daddy's resigned himself, Jeff. I can marry whenever I want with his blessing. And I want to…as soon as we can plan a wedding."

He didn't speak, but gaped at her and for a moment his mouth moved without words. "But…I don't understand. How did you do it?"

"I didn't," she said, tiptoeing to reach his lips. "God did."

Esther crumpled onto her sofa, her mind pitching like a small boat in a storm. Earlier she'd attended church as her father had asked, and lingering in her memory was how Rachel's lovely ring had glinted in the church's soft lighting. God had answered her sister's prayer.

While admiring the engagement ring, her father had accepted the inevitable and kissed Rachel's cheek, giving her his blessing. She and Jeff had invited him for dinner that evening to celebrate.

Esther wasn't celebrating. She sat alone, tormented by memories and pervaded with longing. Disbelief pressed against her heart. She knew Ian had been hurt and angry, but she'd prayed he would call or drop by again. He hadn't.

She rose, headed for the kitchen and turned on the kettle. Pulling a cup from the cabinet, she dropped a tea bag into it and leaned against the counter, waiting for the water to boil.

The house droned with silence and loneliness. She

strode to her office doorway and looked at the chair where Ian had sat…it seemed too long ago.

It had taken forever to admit feelings for him, even to herself. Yet, looking at the empty chair, the empty room, she could barely remember her life without Ian. Being without him seemed impossible.

As she turned back to the kitchen, the doorbell jangled. Gooseflesh rose up her arms. Sunday afternoon. It wouldn't be a door-to-door solicitor. Rachel had plans. It had to be Ian. Her heart rushed to her throat as she darted for the door.

She flung it open, and her heart sank to her toes.

"Hi," her neighbor from across the street, Annie O'Keefe, said, holding a florist's package. The woman had a jacket over her shoulders, and the wind whipped it back, nearly taking it to the ground. She grasped her wrap with one hand and balanced the bouquet with the other. "This was delivered this morning. You weren't home, I guess."

Reeling with disappointment, Esther urged her voice to sound pleasant. "Thanks." She reached out to take the package. "I was at church."

"Well, enjoy," the woman said, tightening the jacket around her and stepping from the porch.

Watching the woman return to her home, Esther waited at the door, clutching the bouquet, the fragrance wrapping around her senses. Jeff, she thought. A thank-you bouquet from Jeff for supporting Rachel.

She looked up at the sky. The sun now hid behind a cloud…a dark cloud…and a brooding wind gusted against the dried leaves along the ground.

She pushed the door closed and heard the kettle whistling in the kitchen. Hurrying toward the sound, she pulled the kettle off the burner, poured the water into the cup to steep and carried the flowers to the kitchen table.

Pulling back the paper, she tore it from the bouquet. Mums, asters and roses embellished with dried autumn leaves. Jeff had good taste. Her thoughts went back to the silk arrangement she'd seen at the craft show. This arrangement looked similar.

As she carried the bouquet into the living room she saw a note card and pulled it out after she'd placed the blossoms on a table. Guessing what Jeff might say, she tore open the card. She expected a single word. "Thanks."

Instead, as she read the neat penmanship, the card—with Ian's signature scrawled at the bottom—trembled in her hand. Tears blurred her eyes, and she followed the misty letters. "Love makes us do strange things. I'm sorry."

Love makes us do strange things. The word *love* leaped from the page and rang in her ears. Did he mean he loved her?

Love. Love. Love. The word multiplied, as did the tears in her eyes. She'd been so quick to blame. So quick to ignore her own part in the charade. So quick to send Ian into the night.

She loved him. She had for months, and, too afraid to admit it, she'd acted like an idiot. She hugged the vase, burying her nose in the flowers' sweet perfume. Ian's citrus-scented aftershave gradually encroached on the aroma and filled her heart.

Reality shot through her. She needed to beg Ian's forgiveness. He'd given her so much in these past months. So much joy, good company and kindness. She'd given him only doubt and fears dragged from her past.

And worse, she'd blamed him totally for the charade. He'd only mentioned it, and she'd captured the idea like a bright butterfly. The ruse had given her opportunities to be in his company, to hold hands, to pretend he loved her, and all the while she'd given him her heart for real.

Shame filled her. She'd acted horribly and longed to ask for his forgiveness. The flowers were his apology—his way of letting her know he loved her.

Esther looked at her wristwatch. Early afternoon. He should be home. She headed back to the kitchen, took a sip of her cooled tea and dialed his number. Counting the rings, she hung up before the answering machine took over.

She sank into a kitchen chair. Now what? Could he be working? He did sometimes on Sundays. Not very often, but it was worth a try. She rose and punched in his direct extension. The line rang and rang, then kicked into voice mail. Esther disconnected.

Pulling out her personal phone book, she flipped to the *B*s. Bay Breeze. She dialed the registration desk. Two rings and a male voice answered.

''Jeff?'' she asked.

''No,'' he said, his voice filled with curiosity. ''This is Jim Mason.''

Memories flooded back. "Hi, Jim, this is Esther Downing. I wondered if you've seen Ian today?"

"Ian's not working today, Esther."

"Oh." She heard her voice ring with disappointment.

"Just a minute," Jim said.

She heard the muffled sound of his hand over the telephone.

"Esther," he said into the mouthpiece. "When he dropped by last night, Leslie said he mentioned sailing today."

Her heart skipped. "Sailing? Thanks, Jim." She pushed the phone onto the receiver and pictured the growing cold and the darkening clouds.

Fear shot through her. Ian may have planned to sail, but surely, if he saw the troublesome weather, he'd have changed his plans. Maybe she'd hung up too quickly. She redialed Ian's number and let it ring until the answering machine picked up. Though she opened her mouth to speak, no words came. She disconnected and dropped into the chair.

A prayer filled her heart. A prayer for Ian's safety and a prayer for God's guidance. She pressed her face into her trembling hands and waited for an answer. What should she do?

With tension mounting, Ian looked into the sky. Dark storm clouds billowed in the north. He'd been distracted, his mind on Esther rather than the weather. It had been a grave error.

He'd left midmorning in the bright sunshine. Though the weather had cooled since the day before,

Ian had felt optimistic. He'd worn a heavy jacket and brought along canvas gloves. But the wind had picked up coming from the north, and the boat had already reached seven knots.

Knowing he'd gone farther than he'd intended, Ian came about, tacking toward the shoreline, only a black line on the horizon. Earlier he'd estimated that he'd passed the city of Holland. Calculating again, he hoped to find the channel at Saugatuck before the storm broke, to wait it out.

With the sky burdened with black thunderheads, darkness came fast, and in the distance lightning zigzagged across the sky, darting into the churning water.

Ian understood weather, but it had changed too quickly, as it often did in Michigan. He feared a squall. Appraising the ominous sky, he wanted to make port before the storm arrived.

The waves swelled, and the boat pitched with the roll of the deep green mountain. An icy spray burst over the deck, and Ian clung to the wheel praying the thunderous front slowed.

When another swell rolled above him and the wind gusted, slapping against the hull, Ian locked the wheel and hurried to the mainsail, attaching himself to a harness and tethering it to a jack line. Reefing early seemed better than waiting until it was too late. Concern pervaded his mind while he shortened the sails, knowing it was worth sacrificing speed for safety. What had he been thinking? He'd always been a good sailor, yet today his mind had been everywhere but on sailing.

The wind had reached gale force, he guessed—at least thirty knots. Another blast howled, whipping the waves higher while the boat rolled and tossed like a roller-coaster ride.

Having shortened and secured the sails, Ian steadied himself, making his way to the cockpit, clinging to the line. When the boat yawed, he lost his footing, but clung to the line to keep himself from falling overboard.

He paused and collected himself. He'd been in storms before. Boats were made to ride out storms. Keeping calm and using safety measures, he'd be okay. The words pierced his thoughts. He pictured Esther's fear and remembered her sorrow over losing her uncle. He wouldn't let that happen to her again.

He stepped forward toward the wheel, but before he reached it, a wall of water rose above him like a black mountain and, with unexpected fury, washed his feet out from under him. As Ian tumbled to the deck, the boat dipped her starboard rail toward the water, and he rolled across the boards toward the angry lake.

Chapter Seventeen

Esther paced the floor, not knowing what to do. Pausing, she stepped to the window and stared up at the gathering clouds. Though the morning had been pleasant and filled with sunshine, now she watched the treetops bend and flutter in the growing wind.

Crossing to the foyer, Esther wondered if Ian had returned to land. Perhaps he had already tied up at the marina. Who could she call? No one. No one at the marina had time to walk the pier to see who was there and who wasn't.

She pulled open the front storm door, feeling a blast of cold wind envelop her in an icy chill. Once more she studied the sky. In the distance dark clouds rolled above the trees, drawing nearer. Ian? If he were sailing, he could be in danger.

After closing the door, she grabbed her coat from the foyer closet, pulled down a scarf from the shelf and found her shoulder bag in the kitchen. She couldn't sit here wondering. For her own peace of mind, Esther knew the marina would be her only source of comfort.

Source of comfort. The words struck her. How easy it was to forget the Lord. How easy to carry the burden of fear on her own shoulders when the Lord had offered to bear the weight.

With her hand fumbling in her purse for her keys, Esther paused. Her prayer rose with the wind, asking God for Ian's safety and for her own trust in Him.

She locked the door and slid into her car. The sunlight had dimmed to a dusky afternoon, like winter when darkness fell over the city before evening. Her hand trembled as she slid the key into the ignition. ''Lord help me to trust in You,'' she said aloud.

Turning the key, she heard the assuring sound of her engine kicking in. She turned on her headlights, shifted into Reverse and backed out to the street. Curious about the weather forecast, Esther snapped on the radio.

Music drifted from the speakers and, frustrated, she punched the buttons, trying to keep her eye on the road. She had no success with the radio, so she gave up and waited. In a moment her favorite station took a break for local weather.

A calm voice sounded over the speaker. ''Heavy winds and falling temperatures are expected for Muskegon County. Small-craft warnings have been issued for boats on Lake Michigan. Severe thunderstorms are predicted from Whitehall to Loving until seven this evening.''

Esther's legs trembled with the news. Not just high winds, but an electrical storm. Only a hurricane could be worse on the Great Lakes. Her pulse galloped as she followed the highway toward the lake. When she spotted the marina, her eyes sought the slips along the pier. She prayed to see Ian's sailboat secured and safe.

The wind sock snapped with unpredictable gusts as Esther left the car and rushed toward the pier. Her heels slammed along the wooden planks, and in the middle of the lengthy wharf she halted, bringing her hands to her mouth to hold back her anguished cry.

Lady Day was gone.

The gusts threw her off balance, and she struggled to retain her footing. Holding back her hair, which was blowing in her face and distorting her vision, she peered toward the impenetrable horizon, praying to see Ian's cutter heading toward the marina.

Red and green channel markers bounced in the distance, riding the billows and plunging into the waves' valleys. Shaking with cold and fear, Esther wrapped her coat around herself and shoved her hands into its pockets.

The first drops of rain hit her like ice shavings, and before she could decide what to do, a shaft of lightning cut through the sky accompanied by a boom that shook the pier and exploded a cloudburst of rain from the black sky. Fear tightened in her chest.

She pulled the hood of her coat over her wet hair and squinted through the downpour, her hopes as damp and dismal as the storm.

"Oh Lord, please. Not again."

* * *

"She's not home," Rachel said, clinging to the handle of Jeff's passenger door, her coat fluttering in the growing wind. "Do you think she went to the marina?"

Jeff shrugged. "I don't know, but get back in the car." He patted the seat.

She slid inside, hugging herself from the sudden chill. "Turn on the heater. Okay?"

He adjusted the car heater and turned on the radio. "There's definitely a storm on the way. I can't believe Ian took the boat out today."

"It was nice this morning," Rachel said, defending him. "Anyway, he's probably back and safe."

"So what should we do? I thought Esther and Ian weren't seeing each other. Why would she be at the marina?"

Rachel drew up her shoulders in disbelief and gave him a how-stupid-are-you look. "When you and I weren't seeing each other, where would you be if you suspected I was out sailing today?"

He gave her a defeated look. "Okay. You're right. I'd be at the marina. Should we go and check it out?"

Rachel thought a moment. Why did she think Esther would be there? Maybe she had gone to the library today. But she suspected that wasn't the case. Not on Sunday. She nodded. "If she's there and worried, I want to be with her."

"Women," Jeff said. "I'm trying to learn this stuff, but I hope you give me a little time."

Hearing his words, Rachel chuckled. "That line sounds familiar."

He grinned and backed out onto the street.

Lightning split the sky and sent a cascade of rain washing along the streets and bending the trees. Rachel kept her hands buried in her coat pockets to hide their trembling. Jeff had made a valiant effort to be more gentle, but tears and emotion seemed to make him uneasy.

Her thoughts shifted to Esther and Ian. In her mind, they seemed a perfect couple—both bookish, both serious and both quiet. Though she knew they had argued, Rachel sensed that the two would solve their differences. She couldn't imagine Esther without Ian at her side. Not anymore.

As Jeff drove, Rachel lifted a prayer heavenward. Though she prayed for Ian's safety, she added a petition for Ian and Esther's reconciliation. God's will would provide.

The rain fell in dark sheets, and Jeff slowed along the road as they approached the marina. Thunder rumbled overhead and lightning ripped the sky in two.

In the parking lot Jeff pulled into an empty spot close to the building. He tugged an umbrella from beneath his seat and hurried around the car to shield Rachel.

She laughed at his attempt to block the rain sailing nearly sideways on the gusts of cold wind that came off the lake. "Forget it," she said, darting from under the protection and heading up the sidewalk toward the pier.

Jeff followed, lowering the umbrella as he ran.

When they reached the pier, Rachel's heart sank.

Esther stood alone in the downpour, a sodden hood clinging to her head like a bathing cap and her arms hanging at her sides.

"Esther," Rachel called as soon as her feet hit the planks. Realizing the rain covered her voice, Rachel gave up the effort and dashed toward her sister.

Esther must have felt her coming, rather than heard her. She spun around, rain soaked and shaking with cold.

Opening her arms, Rachel sped to her side and wrapped her in an embrace.

"Why are you here? Is something wrong?" Esther asked, her voice trembling.

"Nothing's wrong. I guessed you were here." She kept her sister close at her side, remembering so many times that Esther had given her support and comfort. What would she do without her?

Jeff stood nearby, the umbrella once again raised above their heads—a useless activity. He watched in silence.

"Let's go home," Rachel urged. "Standing here isn't doing Ian any good, nor you."

Esther shook her head, sending a spray of rainwater from her hair. "I want to wait for him." She pointed into the darkness toward the faint lights behind the sheet of rain.

Rachel tugged at her arm. "You're shaking from the cold. Please, let's go home. We'll check with the Coast Guard and see if they know anything. Please."

In resignation, Esther faced her, tears streaming from her eyes with the pouring rain. "I want him to know I love him. That's all."

"He'll know soon enough," Rachel said. "And he'll never know if you die from cold."

She placed her arm around Esther's shoulders and eased her along the pier to the warmth of the car. As they reached the end of the pier, Rachel looked over her shoulder, praying along with Esther for Ian's safe return.

Drenched by the frigid lake water, Ian skidded across the pitching deck even though he was tethered to the jack line. The black abyss loomed in front of him while he scrambled to cling to something—lifeline, railing, anything—to keep him from going over the edge toward the inky depths. In the lake he would die in the cold. Alone.

As he flailed, he grasped the tethered harness and caught the rail—saved from the lake for the moment—while Esther's image flashed through his mind. If he survived this horrible storm, he'd rush to her and beg her forgiveness. Pride, rejection, the past. Nothing could stop him.

"Lord, help me," he called into the hellish sky as the boat lurched once more, dipping against the churning waves that washed over him and tearing his aching hands from their hold. As his frozen body swept along the deck, Ian's numbed fingers again grasped the rail while frigid water flooded past him.

He caught his breath, thanking God for His mercy, then, rising to his knees, he clung to the lines and lifted himself to his feet. Nearing the cockpit, he saw the footwell immersed in water from the last angry wave while the bilge pump worked overtime. The water spilled over the deck and past his drenched feet with every roller that lifted the boat and dropped it again.

Ian looked into the dark, stormy sky. Jesus had calmed the sea with two words. *Be still.* The same words struck him. The answer came to him. Stop fighting the wind. He'd never maneuver through the storm and survive without God's help. His only hope was to heave to and wait until it calmed. Better to let the boat make leeway than to resist the wind and rain.

Garnering confidence, Ian worked his way to the winch and dropped the sails as they snapped and fluttered in the wind. Let the cutter find its own position in the waves, he thought, squinting into the rain as he bared the mast, leaving only the storm sail to stabilize the boat. Wave after wave rose and smacked against the hull, spewing water over the deck as he fought to tie the sails securely, fearing they'd be ripped by the wind.

A gust struck the boat as he headed for the cabin. The cutter dipped, but Ian closed his mind to the movement for a moment and inched toward the companionway, his limbs aching and numb.

He dropped down the steps, trembling from the cold, and closed the door. His heart thundered beneath his water-soaked jacket and he pulled it off, then pulled his foulies from a duffel bag. Stepping into his bibbed pants, he lost his footing and clung to the galley counter for balance. When he regained control, Ian slipped on the boots and hooded jacket, then sank to a berth to catch his breath before calling the Coast Guard.

Like a bronco, the cabin pitched and tossed. In his temporary solace from the rain and wind, he prayed a calm would come soon.

"Can't sleep?" Rachel asked.

Esther stopped in the bedroom doorway. "I don't think I've slept at all. I thought I'd try calling Ian again…just one more time," she whispered, not wanting to wake Jeff sleeping on the living-room sofa. Her body ached with exhaustion and fear.

"What time is it?" Rachel asked.

Esther pointed to the glowing clock dial. "Nearly four. Sounds like the storm's let up a little."

"Thank the Lord." Fully clothed, Rachel sat up and slipped her legs over the edge of the bed. "I think I'll make some coffee."

Esther sniffed the air. "I smell coffee. Do you think Jeff's up?"

Rachel chuckled. "He's probably been awake all night. He thinks the best of Ian, and…" Her voice faded.

"I know." Esther lowered her face to her open hand, pressing at the fear and sorrow that pounded in her head. "This is too much like our past, Rachel. Way too much." Her voice trembled as her uncle's image rose in her mind. She drew a quaking breath into her lungs to steady herself.

Rachel reached her side, and they headed for the tempting aroma floating down the hallway.

Esther rounded the corner first into the kitchen.

Jeff sat at the kitchen table, his face strained with a sleepless night, his eyes bloodshot.

"I hope I didn't wake you," he said, his voice rasping with lack of sleep.

"You didn't. I haven't slept much, either," Esther said, heading toward the coffeemaker. "Thanks for making this. I need something to rouse my spirits."

He nodded and took another sip. "There's no news from the Coast Guard."

She swung around to face him. "Did you call again?"

"A few minutes ago. This time I gave them your phone number…just in case they heard something." His face was strained with emotion. "No news is good news. Remember that."

She nodded, knowing the saying could easily have two meanings. No news could mean Ian was safe…but it might also indicate Ian hadn't had time to send an SOS before… She couldn't bear to think the words.

She filled her cup and took a sip before shifting to the phone. "I'll try calling him again." She punched in the telephone number and waited until the answering machine picked up. She disconnected and turned toward them, shaking her head. "No answer."

Rachel patted a kitchen chair. "Come and sit."

Esther crossed the floor and slid into the chair, her thoughts jarring through her mind. When she focused on Rachel, then Jeff, their fearful expressions unsettled her, and her own fright surfaced, causing her cheek to quiver with unspent tears.

"Let's talk about something else," Rachel said.

Talk? No matter what they talked about, Esther's mind was with Ian, but she appreciated Rachel's concern and sent her a faint grin. "You start."

Jeff chuckled, helping to ease the stress for a moment.

"The wedding." Rachel slid her hand over Jeff's. "Let's talk about that."

"That sounds so good to me." He lifted her hand to his lips and kissed it.

"We decided on a spring wedding." Rachel turned to Esther. "Naturally, we want you to be our maid of honor, and Ian..." A deathlike pause fell over the room until Rachel lifted her shoulders with renewed spirit. "Ian will be an usher if Jeff's brother can't make it. He's working out of the country right now."

"If Paul can't get back, I'd like Ian to be the best man," Jeff said, completing Rachel's thoughts.

"That sounds good." Esther's mind whirled, picturing Ian dressed in a tuxedo, next imagining him struggling to survive the icy lake water. Her body jerked from exhaustion. "I'm sorry. I can't sit. I'm too jumpy." She rose while her gaze settled on the refrigerator. "Anyone hungry?" Her stomach churned at the thought, but she needed to do something.

Rachel and Jeff glanced at each other, then returned their attention to Esther. Each gave her an unconvincing nod.

She knew they were pacifying her need to keep busy, but she didn't care. "Keep talking about the wedding, and I'll make us something."

Esther leaned over and pulled a fry pan from the stove's bottom drawer, then set it on the burner. Listening to Rachel talk about flowers and dress colors, she opened the refrigerator and located the butter and eggs. No matter how hard she tried, her mind soared away to the lake. To Ian.

Grasping the ingredients, Esther calmed herself before turning to face her sister and Jeff, who watched her with sorrow-filled eyes.

The telephone's strident ring jolted Esther's senses. Her limbs weakened while her heart plummeted at the sound. An egg splatted to the floor as Esther stared at the infringing machine, frozen in fear.

Chapter Eighteen

Ian took a deep breath, sitting on the edge of the bunk in darkness and thanking God he was still alive and had survived the storm. Though the boat continued to pitch and toss, his senses assured him a new day would bring calmer water.

He eyed his wristwatch. Grateful it was waterproof, he read the dial. Four in the morning. In his struggle, time had flown. He had to get back on deck and read his GPS so he'd know where he was and could radio the Coast Guard he was safe, but his tired and hungry body yearned for rest.

He stepped into the galley and found a nutrition bar. Not bacon and eggs, but better than nothing. He tore off the wrapper and took a bite, then grasped the railing and headed up the companionway to face the weather.

Though the rain had calmed to a drizzle, a strong wind still gusted out of the darkness. Ian paused a moment to gather his bearings. The bilge pump had done its job and the footwell had drained. He read the global positioning satellite unit and noted his location, then radioed the Coast Guard.

On the horizon, faint lights twinkled like distant stars. It was the shore far off in the distance. He sent up a prayer of thanksgiving. Though the waves were still rough, he'd head as close to shore as he could and then wait for a calm to sail into the channel.

With measured steps he moved to the winch, untied the mainsail and grasped the sheet, studying the wind as it caught the canvas. Confident now, he headed back to the wheel, unlocked it and turned his attention toward the distant shore while searching for channel markers.

The water churned and whipped across the forward deck, but Ian didn't let his focus stray. Finally he spotted the lights and guided the boat toward them. Green on port. Red on starboard. He reiterated his father's words. "Red, right, returning."

His father's image rose in his thoughts, and he grinned for the first time in hours, grateful for the training he'd received so many years ago. He pictured his father's rugged, windburned face, his generous smile and strong, steady hands. He hoped that if his father had been watching through the night, he'd been proud.

The picture caught in his mind. If not his earthly father, Ian had no doubt his heavenly Father had guided his craft through the storm. He pictured again Jesus, standing in the boat filled with panicking disciples as He commanded the waves. "Quiet. Be still." Ian said the words aloud.

Startled by his voice in the darkness, he paused, shaken by the sudden hush of the wind. He relished the quiet and tacked toward the channel markers. A gust rose again, but with less violence, and Ian peered into the horizon and saw a flush of orange melding into dawn's deep gray.

Another rising sun and a new day. When he made it to the marina, he had to let his friends know he'd survived. Philip rose in his mind...but Esther filled his heart.

Esther stepped over the broken egg and grasped the telephone. Rachel and Jeff rose as if on springs and stood beside her, ears strained toward her.

Her heart pounded as the man's voice reported the Coast Guard had received a message from Ian. He'd survived the storm and was heading into Saugatuck.

After disconnecting, she turned to the two eager faces and muttered through her tears, "Coast Guard. He's safe."

"Praise God," Rachel said, hugging Jeff with one arm and Esther with the other.

"Where is he?" Jeff asked.

"Heading to Saugatuck." Esther's mind whirred with thoughts. Her deepest desire was to be in Ian's arms.

"Should we drive down?" Jeff asked.

Esther struggled with the desire to say yes, but wisdom said no. When she saw Ian, she had much to confess, much to say to him alone. "No...thanks. I think I'll just wait for now."

Rachel gave his arm a tug. "I think they need some privacy when they see each other, Jeff."

He nodded as if he'd just remembered the tense situation between them. He stood a minute rubbing his forehead. "I think I'll take a ride to the resort. Ian will call Philip once he's in port."

Esther's heart lurched. True. If Ian couldn't make it in to work, he'd notify someone at Bay Breeze. Maybe Philip had learned more about what had happened.

"Want to come along?" Jeff asked her.

She shook her head. "No. You two go ahead." She hesitated. "But would you call me when you know something?"

"Sure thing," Jeff said.

Rachel faced Esther, eye-to-eye, resting her hands on her sister's shoulders. "Are you sure you want me to go? I'll stay here with you and let Jeff go ahead."

"No. Thanks. I'll be fine. I'm beyond fine now that I know Ian's okay."

Rachel slid her hand into Jeff's. "Then we'll call you as soon as we know something. I'm guessing it will be a couple of hours."

Esther nodded and watched them leave through the side door, both looking strained and weary.

Though fatigued to the bone, Esther felt revitalized with the news. God had heard her continuous prayers, and her heart filled with thanksgiving. Eyeing her cold coffee, she sank onto a chair with the cup in front of her, too tired to refill it.

But she wasn't too tired to praise God for His

kindness and for His everlasting guidance. She loved Ian, and she'd pushed him away with her senseless concerns and weak faith. She'd used every excuse to force him from her life, fearing he'd do the same to her.

But God hadn't given up on her and her foolishness, and she prayed Ian hadn't, either. Esther rested her cheek on the table in a mixture of prayer and planning until her eyes closed and sleep overtook her.

Esther jerked awake, and remembered Rachel's promise to call if she heard anything. But she hadn't called.

Esther began to calculate. If Ian had headed for Saugatuck, then when the storm ended and the water calmed he would return to Loving. She figured he'd be back by late afternoon.

Esther gaped at the clock. Nearly four. She'd planned to be at the marina waiting for Ian. She gripped the arm of the sofa, her thoughts flying in all directions. Why had she been so careless? She pushed herself up and swayed before gaining her balance.

Her stomach churned from hunger. The breakfast that she'd thought to make had ended with the early-morning telephone call. Her sustenance for the day had been a few sips of coffee.

She pushed the thought of food aside and hurried toward her bedroom. If she were to meet Ian at the marina, she had no time to spare. After rinsing her face and brushing a daub of makeup on her face, she pulled out clean slacks and a knit top from her closet, then dressed with speed.

Outside the day remained dreary. Clouds still blocked the sun, but the rain had passed and the wind had calmed. She unlocked her car and set out toward the marina.

Esther's mind ached from thought. She'd reviewed her lonely, self-sufficient life many times, comparing it to her new world with Ian. Days filled with fun. Evenings touched by a kiss or a caress. At one time, she'd never cared about those emotions, but having enjoyed her relationship with Ian…having grown to love him, life seemed dreary and empty without him.

God had been faithful, despite her lack of trust in Him. She'd feared sailing for so many years, feared taking a chance on loving because loving opened the possibility of losing someone. Losing her heart.

But that was in the past. She'd lost her heart to Ian already, and she prayed God would give her a chance to beg his forgiveness. A chance to tell him her life would never be complete without him. She prayed Ian felt the same.

Controlling her heavy foot on the gas pedal, she pulled into the marina parking lot. From a distance, she looked down the pier, searching for the sight of *Lady Day*. If Ian had already come and gone, she had no idea what she would do. Would she have the courage to go to his home to plead for his love?

As she neared the pier, disappointment charged through her body. Her feet resounded along the planks, and the thud of her steps matched the pounding of her heart. Ian's boat was tethered in the slip, but Ian was nowhere in sight.

Her emotions seesawed between joy and frustration. Her shoulders drooped, knowing she'd missed his homecoming, missed letting him know how sorry she was for everything she'd done. Here and now she was motivated to tell him the truth—she loved him. If she waited, Esther feared she would lose her nerve.

She knew she was foolish to stand there, staring at *Lady Day*. A chill ran through her, and the cold breeze whipped through her hair. She brushed it back from her face while pulling her jacket more tightly around her with the other hand.

Despite her disappointment, she thanked God for Ian's safety. *Lady Day* looked as sturdy as the last time she'd seen it.

Lady Day. She stepped closer. Her head tilted upward, reading the name emblazoned on the hull. Not *Lady Day*, but *Lady Esther*. Her pulse tripped and longing rolled along her limbs like flames, burning her with desire to see Ian. He did love her. The boat's name testified to that and chased away her prodding doubts.

Fired by the new awareness, she felt courage charge through her again. Today. Tomorrow. Nothing would stop her confessing her love. Nothing.

"Esther."

His voice sailed on the wind and drew her like steel shavings to a magnet. She turned and saw him only feet away.

Ian opened his arms, his tired face filled with hope.

She didn't hesitate, but ran to him, her heart and mind captured in the warmth of his embrace.

Ian's lips met hers, cold to the touch, but heated by the love that needed no words.

"I'm so sorry...for everything," Esther said. "Forgive me."

"Sorry? No. I should beg your forgiveness. I ran off like a scared possum with my tail dragging instead of being honest. I've loved you for...forever, Esther."

His deep affection brightened his eyes, and Esther's world stood still. "I love you, Ian. I've never been so frightened when I thought I'd lost you. Never. But God gave me a kick, and I realized that all I needed was faith. Life is nothing without you."

"We've both been senseless," Ian said. "When I was on the boat—"

"*Lady Esther,*" she said, gazing into his hooded eyes.

He nodded. "Yes...on *Lady Esther.* I realized I'm only a complete person when I'm with you. We were both afraid to take a chance, Esther. Taking chances can hurt. Taking chances can cause sadness. But without taking the step, we have no chance at all to know what love is."

She tiptoed to reach his lips, brushing them with kisses. Kisses so sweet she thought her heart would melt.

As she lowered her heels to the ground, the wind gusted, and a chill ran the full length of her body.

Ian drew her closer. "We'd better get you inside

before you get sick." He nuzzled her head with his cheek. "I'd just called you...but you weren't home."

"I was here waiting for you."

"And now I'm here." He slid his arm around her waist and turned her toward the marina.

As if God said amen, the clouds parted and the sun beamed through the opening, splashing its golden rays along the worn planks and sparkling its diamonds on the churning water below them.

"Hungry?" he asked.

"Only for you," she said, remembering his line from long ago.

"Food now," he said. "We'll talk wedding plans later."

"Wedding what?" she said, her pulse accelerating.

"You don't think I'm letting you get away from me again. *Lady Esther* is a nice name for a boat. But Esther Barry is a wonderful name for a wife."

"Mrs. Ian Barry. I like the sound," she said.

"I love it."

Ian didn't care who would see them through the marina's restaurant window. He paused on the sidewalk and captured her lips with a kiss...a kiss offering the woman he cherished all the love in his heart.

Epilogue

A Saturday in May

"I'm shaking like a leaf," Rachel said, running her hand along the empire waist of her white satin gown. "I think I'm going to cry."

"No tears," Esther said. "You don't see me crying."

Rachel laughed. "You're always in control."

Esther's mind soared back to so many times recently she'd lost total control. "Not always."

"I'll always think of you that way," Rachel said. She paused and raised her hand to Esther's hair. "You look so beautiful."

"Me? You're absolutely radiant," Esther said, giving her sister a hug.

A knock sounded, and Esther stepped toward the bridal-room door and pulled it open. "Is it time?"

Her aunt gave a nod. "Everyone's ready."

Esther smiled. "We'll be there in a minute."

Her aunt gave her a wink and headed back toward the sanctuary.

She looked at Rachel. "It's time."

Time. The word filled Esther's heart. For everything God had a purpose, and today she would witness God's purpose fulfilled. These past months, Esther had seen a new Jeff—quieter, deeper and more devoted to Rachel than he'd ever been.

And she'd seen changes in herself. God had given her peace and assured her that she was truly loved by God...and Ian. She'd renewed her faith and understood God's purpose for her.

Rachel's eyes glistened with excitement and tears as she grasped her bouquet, then handed Esther hers.

Esther opened the door and beckoned to her sister.

Rachel's billowing skirt swished through the door, and when Esther joined her she pressed her cheek to Esther's. "Thank you for being my sister."

Older sister, Esther thought, and for a fleeting moment the troubled days drifted past—their father's ridiculous decree, the matchmaking, the rift with Ian, but in a flash they sailed away on the spring breeze, and new hopes for a miraculous future took their place.

She and Rachel walked together along the corridor. When they reached the narthex, Esther paused, seeing her father waiting for them.

When he saw them, his eyes filled with love and pride.

"You look handsome, Daddy," Rachel said.

Esther touched the boutonniere pinned to his lapel. He did look striking in his tuxedo and bow tie.

"God is good," he said, drawing them closer and kissing each on the cheek. "I only wish your mother could be here."

"She's here, Daddy," Esther said, touching her heart. "Mom's always here."

His smile warmed her soul. Esther had no doubt her mother's love encompassed them all.

The triumphal organ music began, echoing through the arched ceiling. Esther moved to her place beside her father. Rachel stood on the other side.

Looking down the lengthy church aisle, Esther saw Ian and Jeff waiting beside the pastor. Ian looked strong and handsome, his gaze directed at her.

The music grew louder as they neared the front, and Esther gazed into Ian's glistening eyes, bright and unveiled, proclaiming his love and faithfulness.

Catching his breath, Ian observed them approaching, with Rachel in her full sweeping wedding dress, but Esther...he couldn't take his eyes from her. She glided toward him like an angel, her simple gown decorated with beads and pearls glinting in the candlelight. The soft folds of her dress swayed around her slender hips...white satin and lace as pure and delicate as she. Esther. His bride. His wife.

"Who gives these women to be wed?" the pastor asked.

"Their mother and I," their father said, a wistful smile on his face. "Their mother and I."

He stepped aside and sat—alone perhaps, but glowing with love for his daughters.

Pride rose in Ian. Esther had remained strong in her beliefs and had loved her father through all their trials. She'd honored him through it all, and today God's love shone on them. Today she stood before the pastor and guests, willing to be Ian's wife...with both her father's and heavenly Father's blessings.

Rachel and Jeff stepped to the right, their faces beaming with happiness, and Ian linked Esther's arm in his and stepped toward the altar, his spirit soaring.

Esther drew in the familiar scent of fresh citrus mingled with her bouquet of spring flowers. She gazed up at Ian...the man she loved, the man who'd unlocked her world and the man who promised to stand beside her through every joy and sorrow.

God had granted His promise. He encouraged her to open her heart and to accept a new life with Ian. Today with a host of friends and family, she and Ian stood before the Lord united in love.

Two loving hearts blended as one.

* * * * *

*If you enjoyed LOVING HEARTS,
you'll love Gail's story in
next month's Easter anthology,*

*EASTER BLESSINGS:
The Butterfly Garden*

*by Gail Gaymer Martin
Available March 2003
Don't miss it!*

Dear Reader,

No matter where I go in Michigan, I'm no farther than six miles from a body of water—rivers, streams, lakes and the Great Lakes. I suppose that's why I love it so. Nothing is more comforting than watching the sun set on a rippling lake, hearing rowboat oars dip into the water on a quiet night, or feeling the wind in my hair on a boat ride. On my parents' property on the Straits of Mackinac, I spent many summers washed in God's glory of sun, moonlight and water. I suppose this love of Michigan has guided me to set my LOVING series in a small imaginary town on Lake Michigan near Grand Haven. Surrounded by water, my readers will have the opportunity to meet the townspeople, to mourn their sorrows and to rejoice in the blessings that God bestows on them. The story reminds us that in every town we are surrounded by God's love and comfort. We only have to open our eyes to see Him waiting for us to accept it.

Gail Gaymer Martin

Next Month From Steeple Hill's

LONG WAY HOME

BY

GENA DALTON

After a serious injury that ended his career as a bull rider,
prodigal son Monte McMahan returned to the Rocking M
Ranch to make amends with his family and Jo Lena Speirs,
the girlfriend he'd abandoned years ago. Just seeing
Jo Lena stirred up old emotions and made Monte wonder
if it was too late to find love in the arms of the woman
he'd once left behind....

Don't miss

LONG WAY HOME

On sale February 2003

Next Month From Steeple Hill's

SONG OF HER HEART

BY

IRENE BRAND

Norah Williamson had spent her entire life caring for her father and brother, but after their deaths she was left without a purpose. But when she saw a job listing for a therapeutic riding program, Norah knew she had to pursue her long-abandoned dreams. And the owner of the ranch, Mason King, made Norah remember other forgotten dreams...of love and a family all her own....

Don't miss
SONG OF HER HEART
On sale February 2003

Next Month From Steeple Hill's

THE HARBOR OF HIS ARMS

BY

LYNN BULOCK

Now that her husband's killer was back on the streets,
investigator Alex Wilkins was the only man Holly Douglas
could count on to protect her precious family. But as she
began to let Alex into her life—and her heart—she feared
he would unmask her most closely guarded secret.
A secret that was at odds with her strong faith…

Don't miss

THE HARBOR OF HIS ARMS

Book One of the Safe Harbor miniseries

On sale March 2003